I0628910

Young Adult

Fiction

Visit: www.rickstiller.com for more of his books, photographs, and music and www.morgansknot.com for the latest on the Morgan's Knot series.

Morgan's Knot

By

Eric T. Stiller, Jr

Text copyright © 2013 by Eric T. Stiller, Jr.
Cover illustrations © 2013 by Rick Stiller
All rights reserved.
House of the Four Seasons Publishing

ISBN 978-0-9892702-0-5

Visit www.morgansknot.com

For Sheridan,
Ian & Kelly

Morgan's Knot

Nanchez, a hulking giant in a dark uniform and a worn leather apron, stood alone at a long cluttered workbench staring at a large purple *messenger* while twisting a dial on one of the many strange instruments bound together by a tangle of cables. He brushed a stray curl of white hair from his dark eyes with the tip of an enormous finger and muttered, "Right then, it works."

The Keeper of the Dark Powers turned as the lock from the main laboratory hissed open and Jofre strode into the workroom preceded by the staccato of his thick boots clacking a determined cadence and trailing a heavy cape from his shoulders. It was rare for the Grand Master of the Elders to visit this most secret vault unannounced. Usually, Nanchez was summoned at their pleasure, as if he had too little to do in the first place.

The huge Keeper stood, dwarfed by his visitor both in stature and demeanor, and The Master leaned to inquire, "I understand that your calculations proved successful?"

"As if there was any doubt," snarled Nanchez with a twinkle in his eye. There was a certain advantage to maintaining the mystique of the Powers with anyone from the political hierarchy of their society, especially a tyrant who would snuff out a life on a whim.

Jofre rose through the ranks and seized the throne in a short violent coup that only wet his appetite to pursue greater ambitions, "Then you and our *seer* agree?"

The giant Keeper grunted and walked over to remove a cloth covering gleaming metal on another counter, "We've been in agreement for weeks…long enough to prepare a detailed plan and for my engineers to construct this model of a new tunneling machine. It's scaled down, for the moment, because the channel must only accommodate troops and small vehicles. The advantage being that by reducing the quantity of rock that has to be chipped and removed, the excavation will move much more quickly, expediting the mission, and we can always enlarge the duct later, if it proves advantageous."

Jofre's white eyes gleamed as he studied the black diamond claws at the front and a conveyor snaking through the length of the mechanism to ferry debris away from the cut, "Impressive."

"I'm glad you approve because construction on the working version is well underway and tracks are being laid. We should be ready to commence the operation within days."

"Then so be it. I'll consult with the Council but rest assured that you'll have their blessing."

Nanchez turned to stare into the cold white eyes, "Are you sure?"

"We will proceed. Revenge is our destiny," replied Jofre, excusing the Keeper's insolence as sincerity.

"There'll be no stopping, once we've started."

"I'll not be satisfied with simply taking back the rest of the island. No, this is only the beginning. It won't be long before we join with others to dominate all the Powers across the planet."

Chapter Two

Adrian was an ordinary boy waiting in absolute silence in a crush of classmates, watching the second hand on the ancient clock above the entry tick away the final seconds. The first ting of the bell was drowned by the roar of children crashing through the hallowed hallways of the Heritage Academy in celebration of the last day of school for the year. Mired in a rush of bodies, Adrian burst through the heavy oak doors into the warm salty breeze of a sunny afternoon.

He found his best friends, Stubby and Kick, and dashed down the sidewalk through a thicket of parents, charting secret plans for the summer. The pavement gave way to a rocky path, just south of the little village, and they trotted into the forest along the ridge overlooking their homes along the bay.

"I'll call you later," cried Adrian, cutting down the hill through the woods into a flutter of hummingbirds that rose from the meadow to swarm around him like a shawl wafting in the wind, glittering ruby sparkles. Robins, a pair of cardinals, a blue jay, a nest full of wrens in a titter, and a family of squirrels peeked from the branches of a tall maple. A red fox, stalking a clutch of young rabbits through the grasses, stopped to stare, his bushy tail standing straight and still in the gentle breeze, as the lad passed.

The boy banged through the kitchen door to find his mother wearing a yellow bathing suit and a short robe. She leaned for a hug, "Get your trunks on and we'll go for a swim. I have cookies in the basket."

"I'll be right back," said Adrian, racing to his bedroom to change his clothes and scamper back to the kitchen.

They strolled, hand-in-hand, down the pebble beach to a catwalk that stretched into the bay. His father's vintage sloop, The

Sparrow, bobbed gracefully on gentle waves at the end of the dock, elegant lines in gleaming woods and polished brass ready to leap through the waves on the open seas given just a whisper of wind. Adrian peeled off his shirt and plunged into the cold water. He dove deep and exploded through the surface with the sheer joy of his new freedom.

He was tall for his awkward age and a bit lanky. A mop of blond curls fell wet around a tanned face and a few freckles dotted his slender nose. Electric blue eyes sparkled with intelligence and, one might suspect, a bit of mischief, yet there was also a tender spirit barely hiding in a softness at the corners of his mouth.

Sara sat on the edge of the dock, while Adrian swam back and forth, kicking and splashing sheets of cold water that fell just short of her long legs. He laughed at her faint protests and, finally, climbed the ladder to towel himself off. She gazed at her son with pride and poured him a glass of iced tea, opening the small wicker basket to reveal a pile of freshly baked chocolate chip cookies, still warm in a plaid tea towel. Adrian took one in each hand.

"How was your last day of school?"

"It was a waste of time. We'd already finished everything. Besides cleaning out our desks and lockers, there wasn't really much left to do," he mumbled, licking a bit of chocolate from his lip. "I did manage to get a copy of my geography book."

"Did you steal it?"

"No, they were sorting books to be saved for next year or recycled and I asked Mr. Watson if I could have it."

"That's good then. I still have some of my textbooks from college and I actually refer back to them from time to time," smiled Sara. "You never stop learning...although I'm finding that the older I get, the more I have to open up the archives in my mind to find a fact or a name amongst all that's stuffed in there!"

"It's tough getting old, isn't it?" giggled Adrian.

She pursed her lips, feigning offense, "The flip side is that you still have lots of room inside that marvelous mind of yours for reams of information and I, personally, believe that school ought to last twelve months a year, so you don't lose half of what you've learned lolly-gagging around over the summer. That's the way it was when I was a girl."

"That must have been a long time ago," said Adrian, "and I'll bet you had to walk ten miles uphill in a snowstorm every day to school and back."

"Even in the summer!" His mother smirked, "It wasn't quite that bad, I actually liked school."

Adrian was a good student, looking forward to his first year in the upper school. He was fascinated with the process of learning and accepted the challenge, which is not to include the redundancy of the lessons or the repetitive exercises, which were certainly designed to quash any creative brain cells that might multiply inside an inquisitive child's mind. It did not require much effort to earn honors in his classes but his primary complaint was that teachers presented only half the truth.

He was sure there was something deeper, darker, and far more interesting buried in missing articles that must have been omitted to prevent normal people from knowing the truth. There would be time to ponder that notion through the holiday, which fluttered through his mind like a book of empty pages awaiting a dramatic first line.

His mother took his hand in both of hers, sighed, and turned away to stare across the bay. Small waves lapped at the pilings below the dock and gulls gathered overhead, squawking for a morsel. Adrian held a piece of cookie in the air and, one by one, the white birds swooped closer and closer until the bravest snatched a large crumb. Others followed in a small cloud of fluttering wings, their caws growing louder as they jostled for a tidbit.

Sara turned to her son, her eyes somber, "There's something that we must talk about..."

Normally a melody of laughter and mirth, the soft assurance of this particular tenor was reserved for serious matters or apprehension for one of his pranks.

"Dad's been offered...no, ordered to a new job," she said. "The company wants him in Vancouver."

"Vancouver?" stammered Adrian. Vancouver was a very long way from home.

"Yes," she said quietly. "I know this is going to be hard on you. You have your friends, school, and all the things that you've known all your life...but we really have no choice. Your father has interviewed for other jobs and we've decided that this is probably the best decision for all of us."

"But...." sputtered the boy, any words of protest escaping in his confusion. Staring deep into the reflections on the waves below the pier, he watched his dreams for the summer dissipating like the inky ripples spreading from the pilings in perfect iridescent rings. Finally, he asked, "When...?"

"They want your father in Vancouver by September. Between now and then, we have to sell the house, pack and ship our things, and move the boat."

They were quiet for a while as Adrian pondered these unexpected and unwelcome revelations. A huge black raven circled slowly, high above the bay, the golden sunlight reflecting the occasional electric blue-black flash as the enormous bird shifted the feathers at the tips of long thick wings to catch the thermals. He had only seen a few flying over the harbor before, always alone, but certainly none as large and, at this moment, soaring through the clouds represented everything that he was being asked to forfeit.

A gentle puff of wind roused him from his thoughts. He looked at his mother and his eyes filled with tears as he struggled to find the words that might save the happy balance of their life in this tiny hamlet. Sara put her arms around her son and pulled him close, "I know this will be a big change for all of us but we're a family and we'll find a way to make this easier, I promise," she added, her voice trailing off. "There is one more thing,"

Adrian turned, staring expectantly into her blue eyes. She brushed back his hair and kissed his forehead, "Your Aunt Elsie has offered to keep you, while we sail the boat around. Once we're settled, she'll take you to the airport and we'll be waiting when you get to Vancouver."

"But I've been sailing with you and Dad since I was born. I won the trophy in my class the past three years. I could help."

"We talked about that," she said. "If we were not in such a rush, we might agree. After considering everything, we've decided that it would be easier and safer if you spent some time with Elsie, George, and the girls on Morgan's Knot, while we move the boat, find a house, and get things settled. I know that none of this is what you want but it is what we think best."

"When?" Adrian asked, afraid of the answer.

"This weekend," replied his mother, tears flushed her beautiful eyes with sadness and compassion.

Adrian had only visited Morgan's Knot once, when he was younger, and became acquainted with the twins, Molly and Megan, when they visited for a few days, years ago. They were nice enough but certainly not the friends he hoped would share his summer.

"You'll like the island," his mother said with a gentle, knowing smile. "It's a very magical place. I grew up there and I know that you'll learn how special it is, if you'll give it a chance until we can send for you."

Adrian did not reply but slumped off the dock into the cold water and let himself sink into darkness before stroking hard into the open bay. Finally, shivering and depressed, he swam back to his mother and dried himself off. Before she could stand, he darted across the gangway and up the hill into the woods without looking back. His heart felt abandoned, confused, angry, and an irrepressible sadness.

There was no one that he could talk with who might soothe his anguish or change their decision. Everyone else in the little hamlet was staying, some with family trees stretching back to the Vikings or so they claimed. People didn't move in and out of the village. They were born here, lived here, and died here. They might go away to college or to follow a dream but they always came back.

A thin layer of clouds shrouded the sky, muting the glittering reflection of the sun on the water silhouetting several sailboats moored to buoys in the harbor that opened into the Atlantic. His eyes traced every detail of the only home that he had ever known. A screened porch wrapped around the south side beneath gray wood shingles and yellow shutters almost glowed against the blue clapboard cottage nestled beneath several huge maple trees. The first pink blossoms had opened on his mother's rose bushes, standing determined despite waves of cold north wind that refused to give way to summer.

He etched the view into his memory because he felt in his heart that he might never see it again, then turned and scampered up the path through the woods until he was out of sight. He slumped down next to the trunk of an ancient oak and sobbed uncontrollably, knowing that the roots of his life, the village that was the foundation of his identity, would be displaced by a boring summer on Morgan's Knot with cousins he hardly knew and then a new life in Vancouver. "Somehow, someday, I will come back."

He was roused by the distant caw of the gigantic raven tracing long slow circles in the sky over the bay. A patch of sunlight, streaming through the giant trees, illuminated the tiny meadow of wildflowers. Waves of hummingbirds fluttered into the air, wrapping him in a cloud of buzzing wings and a chorus of tiny chirps, their joy lifted him from the ground and guided him along the path to the little blue cottage.

Sara took the helm and guided the bow of the beautiful sloop into a strong north wind under clear blue skies, while Adrian and his father raised the mainsail and then the jib. John was tall and broad shouldered, with dark hair and eyes. Born of a nautical family, he had been a naval captain during his service before becoming a ship designer, although racing yachts were a not-so-secret passion. His movements around the deck were comfortable and easy from years on the seas and he taught his son to read the winds and the waves, to find his way by the angle of the sun, and to feel the rhythm of a sailboat.

The Sparrow passed through the jetties into a choppy sea but leaned into her keel, slicing her way with ease. Adrian relieved his mother at the tiller and asked, "How long?"

"We'll be there by sunset," replied his father, who was studying his own personal charts. Adrian loved piloting the sloop. He looked up at the sails and leaned into the tiller to gain just a little more speed. He wanted to protest that he was sailor enough to make the journey but he knew their decision was final. There was the temptation to look back at the house and the cove, life as he had known it since the day he was born, but he knew that it would just make leaving harder and he stared straight ahead into the open sea. Waves of blond hair blew in tangles around his face, veiling tears streaming down his cheeks.

As the sun settled to the horizon in the west, his mother sat down beside him with a knowing smile, her long slender fingers closed around something that glistened. "I have a very special gift for you," she said. "I think you'll find it useful on Morgan's Knot."

She opened her hand to reveal a golden key, somewhat larger than an old-fashioned house key, with a large square where the teeth might have been. The rectangle contained a perfect cross, even on each side, surrounded by a slender crescent etched through the metal. A tiny star floated near the breach at the top, as if trying to escape into the freedom beyond the confines of the inverted arch. The spinnaker billowing over the bow of The Sparrow bore the same cross and crescent, a tribute by John to his wife's ancestry. Adrian reached out and took the key, examining it with a quizzical look.

"I think that you'll find this valuable," she said. "I did when I was younger."

Adrian thought the well-worn key was beautiful. It had been handled and used through so many years, the metal was worn to a smooth patina with no hard edges. He had no inkling of the function or significance and stared at her with curiosity in his eyes.

"As I said, Morgan's Knot is a magical place and this key will open doors of understanding for you. You'll see. Keep it with you wherever you go." Without another word, she stood to peer across the waves, "There it is!"

Adrian spied a large black lump on the northern horizon. It had been years since he last visited and he remembered little about the place, "I've always wondered, why is it called Morgan's Knot?"

"I wanted you to see it at sunset," she said pointing to the black mountain, a jagged cone of rock jutting into the evening glow above the northern end of the island. "If you watch right up there in the rocks on the mountain, you'll see."

As they tacked closer and the sun melted across the horizon, the black rocks began to glow in reflection, their brilliant facets bleeding crimson and gaining shape. Slowly, the peak was transformed, bound in massive ropes tied in a heavy knot with the leads flowing away around the summit.

"It really does look like a knot," exclaimed Adrian. He noticed that the peak above the glowing stones appeared capped by snow but thought it another play of light. "Who was Morgan?"

"He was the man who discovered this island and brought the families to live here generations ago. That's only the beginning," smiled his mother, kissing him on the forehead. "There's so much more."

"Sara, you take the helm while we pull down the sails," said John, as he guided the sloop into a small cove from the southeast. Several fishing trawlers were tied up along the wharf and a little village rose up a hill beyond the waterfront. On the only open dock, Adrian's cousins and his aunt and uncle, George and Elsie, waved with excited anticipation.

John took the tiller and guided The Sparrow to the pier, while

Adrian and Sara threw lines to George and the girls. "Bumpers out!" cried John, as the beautiful sailboat glided to rest within inches of the pilings beneath the dock.

John lifted Sara onto the wharf and into her sister's waiting arms. Adrian grinned at the two women, so much alike with their fair complexions, blond hair, and blue eyes. Elsie was a bit shorter than his mother and not quite as slender but they shared a wonderful sparkle that infected everyone around them.

George reached a hand to pull Adrian onto the dock and enveloped him in a hug. He was tall, with strong, thick arms and large hands, rough from physical work. His huge, dark eyes twinkled behind tiny glasses, which seemed to pinch his face into a squint as he leaned down to the boy. "It's lovely to have you here," he said with a warm smile, clapping his nephew on the shoulder. Brushing his salt and pepper hair back from a tan and weathered brow, he replaced a well-worn felt hat and rose to shake hands with John and hug Sara.

Adrian turned to greet his cousins, Molly and Megan, who were a year younger. Both had long blond curls surrounding rather round faces framing those same blue eyes. Molly's smile was warm and friendly and she seemed genuinely delighted to see him. Megan gave him a little smirk and a brief hug but her eyes bored into him, rummaging through his soul for hidden flaws.

Adrian jumped back into the boat to help his father stow the sails and close the hatch, while George and the girls carried their bags to what appeared a small truck. Unlike any vehicle that he had ever seen, there was an open cab under a short awning, a steering wheel in the middle above a long bench seat, wheels made of wood and covered with a metal flashing instead of rubber tires, and spokes like those on an old-fashioned wagon or cart. There was no bulge of an engine compartment in front of the cab and there certainly was no horse to pull it along.

George climbed behind the wheel with Sara and Elsie on either side, while the twins made room for John and Adrian in the back.

Without a sound, the truck leapt into motion and climbed through the small village to a ridge that crested onto a great open plain. Small cottages dotted the landscape, their windows glowing as the last wisp of the setting sun slipped behind a forest, silhouetted in the distance along a jagged ridge that crawled along the length of the island to the south.

Between houses, fields in various stages of plowing, planting, and harvesting formed a checkerboard of textures separated by narrow lanes overhung with graceful old trees, lush and green with the new growth of spring. To the north, the black mountain jutted ominously into an inky sky, a gargantuan lump of fragmented rock that must have exploded from the very core of the Earth to attach itself to the rest of the island in some ancient upheaval. It seemed much more imposing than it appeared from the boat and Adrian felt a chill run down his spine as he gazed up at the indigo glow on the snowcap.

Molly and Megan were identical twins and he was sure they would be unmerciful if he mixed up their names. As they talked excitedly, he noticed that Molly always looked directly into his eyes when she spoke in a rapid-fire gush, while Megan tended to look away, as if pondering her words. "As long as they're talking, I'll be able to keep them straight," thought Adrian.

It was dark by the time they arrived at the old stone farmhouse. The truck purred to a stop and Elsie slid from her seat, pointing to the two lamps on either side of the door, which spilled warm amber down the staircase. George and John grabbed the bags from the back of the truck as the group hustled up the steps into the house and Adrian noticed a small brass plaque to one side of the heavy oak door that read, "The House of the Four Seasons."

"Come in, come in," said George, as the door closed silently. Elsie walked through the front hall and turned left into the kitchen, pointing at lamps as she passed. Each flickered to life, as if she had pressed some invisible switch.

Molly grabbed Adrian's hand and pulled him to the staircase, "Come on, we'll show you to your room."

Megan produced a round glass ball, about the size of a grapefruit, "You'll want this." He took the globe carefully and it glowed bright blue. "Don't worry, you won't break it," she laughed. "It's called an *orb*."

The girls bounded up the stairs to a landing completely encircled by heavy wooden doors.

"Do you have a key?" asked Megan.

Adrian reached into his pocket and withdrew the golden key that his Mother had given him on The Sparrow. Molly laughed as he held it up and led him to a burl wood door at the far end of the hall, "Put the key in the lock, but don't turn it."

Adrian inserted the key into a slot beneath the doorknob and, through force of habit, began to spin it. A deep, mysterious voice resonated from the door or, perhaps, behind the door, "Oooo, that tickles!" Adrian instinctively released the key and jumped back in alarm. The girls doubled over in laughter.

"Ah, that is a key that I have not felt in many years. Is it you, Sara?"

"No, I'm Adrian, Sara's son," he replied, feeling odd speaking to a door.

"Welcome, Adrian," said the voice, as the door heaved open. Adrian took the key from the latch and slipped it into his pocket. He held up his *orb* and two strange round lamps painted the room in warmth.

Chilled air shrouded him like the first breath of winter, as he stepped through the threshold but a bright fire sparked to life in a small stone fireplace at the foot of a large room, with a curved beamed ceiling and a four-poster bed at the far end. A soft chair sat near one of two windows, a writing desk nestled between them, and a small dresser rested against the wall near another door on the left.

"The bathroom is through there," explained Megan, pointing at the second door, which opened as she gestured.

Adrian put his bag and the *orb* on the bed. The glowing ball dimmed as soon as he put it down. He looked around the room and then to his cousins, who were giggling at his expression. "Your mother did tell you that this was a magical house, didn't she?" they asked in unison. He nodded in response, his mouth slightly agape.

"Well, this is just the beginning. Once the house knows who you are and that you're supposed to be here, it won't ask you to produce your key again. If you want to light a lamp, just point at it," said Molly. "Our room is next door, c'mon."

The *orbs* brightened the darkened hallway as they turned to the door next to Adrian's room, which opened with the greeting, "Good evening, girls!" Molly raised her hand to light the darkened room, which was slightly larger than Adrian's, with two beds, two dressers, two small desks, and two overstuffed chairs. A large bookcase crammed with books, most worn as if they had been handled and read many times, covered most of the window wall.

The beds were piled with stuffed animals and ribbons and bows in every imaginable color fluttered like butterflies on long streamers that curled around the bedposts. A pair of small night tables nestled between the beds, stacked with books and notebooks, and, at the far window, a small telescope was pointed at the sky.

Adrian wandered over to inspect an *orb*, several times larger than those they carried up the stairs, and as he reached out, a blue light radiated around it. A voice from within asked, "Where would you like to go this evening?"

Adrian jumped, shooting a quizzical look at his cousins, who chuckled. "You have television and videos and the internet, don't you?" asked Molly.

"Yes," replied Adrian, still hesitant.

"Well, this is television, the telephone, and the internet all wrapped up in one," said Megan, impatiently. "We can watch entertainment, or listen to music, or do research for school, or talk to our friends with this. We call it a *messenger.*"

"Here, I'll show you," said Molly. She turned to the *large orb* and said, "Cartoons!" and it flickered with a radiance that surrounded it like a blue cloud. Suddenly, Bugs Bunny appeared, yammering madly, bouncing from one side of the image to the other, his figure flashing through midair in front of the *orb*.

Fascinated, Adrian stared at the cartoon, the image so crisp and real that he was overwhelmed by the sensation that he could almost snatch the rabbit out of the video. "Oh, we've seen that one a hundred times," cried Molly. "I'm hungry, let's go see what's for dinner!"

Megan turned to the *messenger* and said, "Good night." As suddenly as it had appeared, the image dissolved and the glow faded.

Adrian followed the girls into the hallway and the lights dimmed and the door closed silently. He held the *orb* high, illuminating the entire passage, "Why don't you just have lamps in this hallway?"

"Oh, it's Mother. She says that they've been doing it this way for generations and there's no reason to change now," replied Molly.

"I think it's her special reminder of the magic of this place. We get so used to things being the way they are that we take it all for granted," added Megan.

"Why are there so many doors?"

"Well, it is a magical and hospitable house. In spite of the size on the outside, each door leads to at least one bedroom and a bathroom. It sort of expands to accommodate lots of guests."

"That's incredible."

"Yeah, but it's true!" laughed Molly.

They clamored down the stairs and Adrian noticed his father and George sitting together in front of a large fire in the hearth in the parlor. The children dropped their *orbs* in the carrier in the foyer and marched through a doorway to find their mothers working in a large, old-fashioned kitchen with an oval table to one side. "Ah, there you are," said Elsie. "Dinner will be a few minutes. We've made some treats to hold you over. Girls find Adrian something to drink and take these to your father and John. And don't spill!"

The twins poured apple juice into three glasses from a bottle from the refrigerator and Megan carefully carried a small tray of toast points covered with tomatoes, herbs, and cheese into the living room.

As they crossed the hallway, Adrian again felt that chill but the fire warmed the lounge nicely. She placed the tray on a low table in front of the men and giggled, hesitating for a moment to be polite before grabbing a piece of toast and munching hungrily.

Adrian gazed around at the fine comfortable furniture, overstuffed bookcases surrounding the fireplace, and a credenza on the far wall with three fading portraits of two women and a man in simple black frames. He walked over to gaze at the two women, one looked a bit like Elsie with darker hair but the other bore no family resemblance. The man in the center frame had fair skin, straight black hair, and intense but kind eyes that seemed to peer out through the years, judging or challenging whoever dared look at the image. It was an inviting room but there was certainly nothing that even hinted at magic, other than *orbs*, *messengers*, and talking doors.

"That's quite a journey that you'll be making," said George. "Are you sure The Sparrow's up to it?"

"Oh, I'm sure we'll be fine. We've got the radio, so we can stay in touch and we're just heading into hurricane season but the southern Atlantic hasn't had time to heat up yet. I've been meaning to upgrade the electronics but the old ways have worked this long. We talked about selling her and buying another when we get there but she's been in the family for generations so I'd hate to give her up," said John. "She's an old friend and she'll look after us."

The sisters wandered into the room with another small platter, chatting about friends and family, catching up on life on the island. It had been several years since Sara was last home and Adrian knew that his parents were planning to leave in the morning. "Dinner will be ready in a few minutes," said Elsie, as she passed the tray.

After a feast accompanied by stories and laughter, the men carried the dishes to the kitchen, while Sara took Adrian's hand and led him out the back door. A soft breeze bearing the scent of a salty sea wafted across the island, as they stepped into the warmth of a summer evening to sit together on a split log bench at the bottom of the steps. Sara put an arm around Adrian's shoulders and pulled him to her, "I know this is awkward but I also know that you'll love it here. I see that you've already discovered the *orbs*. Did you use your key?" she asked.

"Yes, and the door talked to me!" he said. "It asked if I was you."

"Well, it was my key when I lived here."

"But the voice? And the *orbs*? And the *messenger*?" Adrian looked into his Mother's soft eyes, her smile was gentle and loving.

"I told you, this is a magical place," she said. "These are only a few of the wonders that you'll encounter. Things happen differently here and there are powers that our ancestors mastered that don't exist in the rest of the world, which is too bad. You'll meet Professor Ponte soon enough, he's the astronomer, teacher, and Keeper of the Powers."

"I should apologize for not preparing you for all of this but…there just isn't any way to explain it, unless you're here," she paused, "and, in a way, I think I'm guilty of shielding you from it.

We think that our trip will take six to eight weeks and then another few to get things settled in Vancouver. We'll send for you as soon as we can," said Sara, looking into her son's teary eyes. "In the meantime, enjoy this wonderful place. You seem to like the girls and I know that Elsie and George will care for you just as I would."

"But…" Adrian's words trailed off as a large tear leaked down his cheek. His Mother pulled him closer and they were quiet for a while. Adrian could feel gentle sobs ripple through her warm body and he was comforted by a faint hint of perfume that smelled like spring flowers. He didn't want this moment to end…but it did.

Chapter Three

It was bright and sunny with a brisk north breeze, as a glum Adrian stood on the dock with Elsie, George, and the girls. The Sparrow slipped through the mouth of the little harbor and the boy could not pull his eyes away from his mother and father, who were both looking back, waving, and trying to smile. He turned away to hide his tears and wished the coming weeks would pass as quickly as the preceding evening.

The Sparrow cleared the jetty into open water and Adrian watched the sails billow as she caught the wind, listed to starboard, and picked up speed. It seemed only moments before the huge mainsail dwindled to a faint white fleck swallowed in the reflections skittering across the cold blue sea. George gathered the children and herded them into the 'trolley' as he liked to call the odd-looking truck. Adrian sat in the back, facing the water, as they climbed through the village. The girls seemed to sense his sadness and sat quietly beside him.

"Godspeed", he thought, as the tiny white sail vanished in the distance. He let his eyes roam around the village and noticed there were no people wandering among the shops. The trawlers, tied up at the docks, were in exactly the same positions as the previous evening. There was no movement, no sign of life in the hamlet.

The path opened into a plain that stretched to the base of the black mountain. Adrian noticed the white streak at the top of the peak. "Is that snow on the mountain?"

Megan replied, rather curtly, "Yes."

"But it's warm enough to melt the snow, how can that be?"

"As we said, this is a magical place. I think we should let Dad explain it to you. He'll be wanting to have a chat when we get home, if I know my father!" said Molly.

"No satisfaction there," thought Adrian, absorbed by visions of his parents, his home, a long adventure on The Sparrow that he would not share, and his reluctant curiosity about life in Vancouver.

As the trolley bumped through the gate, Adrian lifted his eyes to take in the farm. The sun was high in the east and the old stone house sat on a plateau sweeping out from the ridge, above a bluff jutting out of the ocean, surrounded by fields and gardens bordered by ancient gnarly oak trees that arched over cart paths running between the meadows. He noticed an old mule pulling an ancient plow through the field on his left. There was no one behind the plow and the mule seemed to be doing the work without human direction. He looked at the girls, the question in his eyes.

"Oh, that's just Bessie. She's plowed that field so many times over the years, she resents anyone trying to guide her," said Molly.

Megan added, "You'll notice that the animals act differently here. There's no hunting…rather an understanding between the animals and the humans. We help each other. Dad calls it a symbiosis. The meat that we ate last night for dinner was brought in from the mainland."

"We produce just about everything we need and we couldn't do that without the help of the animals who share the island with us. Sheep produce wool and there's cotton growing on the south end of the island, so we have fibers for clothing. The bees make honey, which they share with us, and they pollinate the plants. The chickens produce eggs and the cows and goats give us milk to make butter and cheese. Each animal has a job, just like people. We care and provide for them and they help us in return. It's called The Balance."

"Even the snakes!" giggled Molly. "They chase the chickens out of the garden, and root out mice and moles tunneling underneath."

"The only stipulation is that we do not eat the animals who live here. That would be like cooking your best friend!" said Megan emphatically.

"Isn't that sort of…hypocritical?"

Megan stared defiantly, certain that he was the stupidest boy on the entire planet, "Humans grew big brains when they became carnivorous. Some of us can exist on a vegetarian diet but most need some animal protein just like the tiger or the shark."

Molly smiled, "We eat a very balanced diet supplemented mostly with fish but occasionally real meat. I'm sure my father will explain it to you."

Adrian turned to the vegetable garden across the path from the kitchen. Honeybees rushed back and forth through the garden to beehives at the corners, butterflies flitted from plant to plant, and birds flew in and out of the foliage, plucking bugs and rising into the air with happy caws.

He noticed that the vegetables at the south end of the garden were covered with young tender shoots, while those to the north were more mature. He gazed out over the fields surrounding the old farmhouse and found those in the east had the pale lime color of new growth. The patches to the south were a deep rich green, spotted with the colors of fruits, vegetables, and flowers. To the west, he saw autumn shades of rusty red and gold.

George pulled the trolley up to the kitchen door and Elsie said, "Come along children and we'll have some lunch."

Molly cried, "I'm hungry!"

"You're always hungry!" replied Megan.

"I know but I'm especially hungry now!"

Megan caught up with her mother, who was bustling up the steps to the front door, "The kids are going swimming this afternoon, can we go?"

"Certainly! It will be a good opportunity for Adrian to meet some of your friends. Run down to the cellar and fetch a jar of honey for your sandwiches."

Adrian followed the girls around to the north side and down a flight of stone steps to a cellar beneath the house. The heavy door creaked open and Molly pointed to the *orbs* hanging from the ceiling. A gentle glow rolled from the doorway to the back of the room over row upon row of shelves from floor to ceiling, each filled to overflowing with mason jars containing every type of food imaginable. Awed by the sheer volume, he wandered farther back into the room and discovered baskets of vegetables and fruits, bins of potatoes, onions and garlic, larger urns filled with grains, sugar, and flour, and small jugs of honey, jams, molasses, and peanut butter. At the far end of the vault, he spotted four doors glowing cold blue, the glass frosted with a thin layer of ice. "Those are the freezers," said Molly, grabbing a jar from a shelf. "They're full of fish and meat and things that can't be stored or canned."

The children turned to leave and Megan said, "Good night!" The *orbs* dimmed, as they climbed the steps, and the door closed behind them. Adrian looked to the north where the fields were barren. His gaze drifted up to the cold black mountain that dominated the northern horizon. Storm clouds gathered around the precipice, although the sun was warm and bright at The House of the Four Seasons. In spite of a gentle summer breeze, a chill ran down his spine and the hairs at the back of his neck prickled.

He noticed a tall slender rock rising alone, about halfway between the farmhouse and the mountain, growing from the plain like a crooked black finger pointing into the sky. A metallic cap, like a bloated silver thimble, glinted in the sunlight at the top of the pillar.

After lunch, George asked Adrian to join him in the study, which was tucked behind the staircase and rich with fine wood paneling. Shelves stuffed with books covered the walls and a small fire crackled in the fireplace beside a door that opened to the north. There was frost on the glass.

George motioned for Adrian to sit in one of two large wingback chairs before the fire. The boy sat on the edge of the oversized chair while George poured two cups of tea from a silver service on a small table and said, "I don't know how much your mother told you about Morgan's Knot but I take it that you've noticed that things here are a little bit...different?"

"She said that this was a magical place," replied Adrian, "but she didn't really explain it."

"Well, it is rather hard to explain," said George with a soft and gentle smile. "You'll have noticed the plaque by the front door?"

"The House of the Four Seasons?"

"Yes," said George. "This is the House of the Four Seasons. There are places on Earth where the rules of nature don't follow what we perceive as normal conventions. This is one of them. To those who approach or enter this house through the front door, everything seems as it should…but there are four other doors, each facing one of the four points of the compass. If you leave the house through any of those doors, you'll find that each leads to a season. The east door takes you to spring, the south to summer, the west to autumn, and," his Uncle pointed to the study door, "north to winter. If you go out one door and I go out another, we'll not find each other because we're in different seasons. Time is a bit skewed."

Adrian looked up at his uncle's smile, not quite sure whether he was joking, but George's grin could not mask the sincerity in his wise old eyes.

"You'll also have recognized that the *orbs* that give light, the *messengers*, the doors that speak to you, and the trolley that seems to run without a traditional engine, are different than normal light bulbs, televisions, or automobiles to which you are accustomed."

"Yes," replied Adrian, a bit bewildered.

"Morgan's Knot is blessed with a power source that allows us to use these things without wires or generators. Each of the houses that grace this island has a unique set of properties. Several, like ours, sit at a point where the seasons overlap which permits growing crops at a fantastic pace twelve months a year. Others, like the doctor's house, are built over a spring that has rather amazing healing properties, or Samuel's foundry, which has a vent that produces intense heat for metalworking."

"Each home site was chosen for it's powers and each of those points sits on a vector from the main power source that we call the Crystal. I'll leave the science of it to the Professor. You'll probably meet him tomorrow night, as the girls have an astronomy lesson."

"Do these 'Powers' exist in other places?" asked Adrian.

"Yes," said George with a knowing smile. "I'd be willing to bet that you could go through the history books, after our talk, and pinpoint those sites around the world. They are those places where civilizations rose from insignificance and raced ahead of the technologies of their times. Unfortunately, those chapters of history also reveal that many of those empires eventually vanished, most without leaving an explanation for their sudden demise. They became out of balance with the laws of nature."

"Balance?" inquired Adrian.

"Yes, we call it The Balance, the equilibrium between man and nature. That's one of the reasons we don't hunt or slaughter animals, although we do eat meat and fish, which is necessary, if hypocritical. Those things that we do not produce on the island are shipped in on one of the trawlers that you saw at the docks and once each month the fishing boats go out to very specific places to fish. The sea creatures allow us one day and no fish are taken that are not consumed."

"As long as The Balance between man and nature is maintained and we don't draw too much power from The Crystal, these seemingly magical properties will continue to provide us with everything we need. The magic of Morgan's Knot isn't the stuff of fairytales and legends, it's a practical gift from Mother Earth that we must protect."

"How many people live on the island?" asked Adrian.

"It varies. At times, there are as few as six or eight hundred to as many as a several thousand living on our part of the island. Every child goes to school, just as you do. They learn all the traditional subjects that children are taught in a normal curriculum, but they also study the Powers of this place and how to use them in a positive way. Every adult on the island has gone to a university on the mainland and every child will go when their time comes."

"Most go on to receive upper level degrees. Mine was in engineering. The Doctor's was in surgery and Eastern medicines. The Professor has several degrees, some of which still bewilder me. Your mother left to attend university and fell in love with your father, who was serving in the Navy. She chose to live a normal life with him on the mainland rather than returning here. Others bring their spouses back to live on the island. It's a choice that each of us has had to make. I was fortunate to fall in love with Elsie when we were very young. We were far enough removed in the family tree to marry."

"You said 'our part of the island'?"

"You'll have noticed the mountain to the north? There's another group of people living on the far side of it. Generations ago, there was a schism...a group of families wanted to harvest the power of the Crystals to enrich themselves. They wanted to sell the power and develop the island as an exclusive haven for the wealthy.

As history has shown, when The Balance is disrupted, the power is lost forever. Our ancestors banished those families to the north side of the island. Since then, there has been very little contact between the two groups. We see their ships going to and from the mainland and, occasionally, we pick up news of them from our suppliers."

"How was this island discovered?" asked Adrian.

"Generations ago, those who believed in The Balance of Nature were branded as pagan worshippers and witches. Thousands were accused of heresy and many were tortured and killed. During that period, Morgan, who was the captain of a trading ship, stumbled upon this island. He realized that the glowing crystal knot on the mountain was evidence of the Powers that his family elders described when he was a child. He withheld it from his charts and returned to port, where he gathered twenty-four families of believers. On a cold moonless night, he loaded them onto two ships and sailed out to this island, never to be heard from again."

"As time passed, they harnessed the power of The Crystal to

provide everything they needed. They found the vector points and built their homes to suit their individual talents. Other than those few things that we import from the mainland, we have no need for money. We have everything that we could possibly want."

"But where did it all start? Who was the first to master these powers?" asked Adrian.

"The histories can be traced back to the dawn of man but our first recorded history starts in…well, you've heard of Atlantis, I presume?" inquired George with a twinkle in those large dark eyes dancing behind his tiny glasses.

The sun hung low in the west, as the last of the tall ships dropped anchor and lowered enormous sails, rocking regally on gentle waves. Twelve magnificent trading vessels lined up just outside the mouth of the harbor, bows to the sacred mountain rising like a giant cone at the center of the port. Arched bridges joined rings of atolls to the mainland at the four points of the compass within a deep channel bounded by natural jetties that formed a colossal crescent, its arms encompassing a protected refuge from storms that rolled in from the sea. A tiny island guarded the narrow passage, bounded by a stone seawall that formed a six-pointed star and manned by emissaries of the Royal Family who kept detailed records of each ship that sailed in or out of the Kingdom, their port of origin, their destination, their cargo, and those traveling aboard. The traders moved to their patrons through concentric grand canals deep into the heart of the capital but invading warships would find no direct or unprotected course.

A large step pyramid rose at the foot of the mountain, its position carefully aligned with the sun and the stars to act as a living calendar that marked the time of day, the changes of the seasons, and the movements in the heavens. Red tile roofs of the twin Temples of Wisdom and Knowledge rose from towering columns on either side of a broad stone plaza that swept down a flight of grand terraces to the water.

The ancient people imported white stone for the construction of the first sacred temples and all public buildings were erected in a similar method and style, which provided a beautiful and functional metropolis where the population could live in harmony with their natural surroundings. The white city glowed in fading sunlight that brushed the sky with strokes of the hot oranges of firelight fading to inky blue in the east.

Jofre, the most powerful merchant in the trades and, perhaps, the richest man in the kingdom outside the Royal Family, was master of this fleet and several more. He took pleasure in applying his power and flaunting his wealth and those who had been invited to join this armada felt privileged to be included at the fringes of his vast and elite inner circle.

Each ship was loaded with exotic food and drink, far more than the guests could consume in a week, but no guest of Jofre ever left feeling disappointed or less than full. Servants passed golden trays bearing delicacies from the far reaches of the trading world and a quartet played softly on the stern of Jofre's largest ship, the Sophia, named after a daughter who died in infancy.

"It won't be long before they kindle the lights," said Alius, who was reputed to be the most beautiful and desirable of the maidens in the upper echelons of the merchant society. Her older brother, Demetre, was the Captain of this trader, the Jasmine, and her younger brother, Simian, a scribe who worked for the Master *Seer*, Modulus. It was considered a great honor to be a scribe, because very few of the population possessed the special gift of interpreting the characters in the Book of Wisdoms or its dark sister, the Book of Knowledge.

Alius chided her younger brother, "Must you carry your work everywhere you go, Simian? This is a festival, a time to enjoy this very special moment."

"Modulus instructed each of us to take our books with us

tonight and not to let them out of our sight. I don't know why. Personally, I think he's paranoid that Nanu is going to burn down the city or something!"

Nanu, Keeper of the Powers, discovered a method to produce light without a flame and this was to be the unveiling of his greatest triumph. The island, usually dark at night, save the torches along the streets and fires and oil lamps that glowed within the homes, was to be illuminated by Nanu's new invention.

Guests settled on large pillows scattered around the decks and Simian spotted several co-workers on other ships. He waved excitedly to Protus, his best friend and fellow scribe, on the beautiful trader bobbing along side the Jasmine. Each vessel was crowded with the family and friends of the captains, in addition to those invited at Jofre's personal behest. There were perhaps seventy-five people on Demetre's ship, more on Jofre's newest and largest vessel, the three-master.

Simian gazed around at the people lounging on the deck, the influential core of their culture - the finest artisans, merchants, doctors, shamans, and political leaders, representing all of the powerful and prominent who were not required to participate in the ceremonies on shore.

As the setting sun touched the horizon, the peak of the mountain began to glow crimson in reflection and the people on the boats, as well as those on the shore surrounding the harbor, cheered in anticipation of darkness. Torches along the streets in the city appeared as tiny glowing embers flickering across the waves like glowing filaments from a spider's web in a gale.

Presently, the last glimmer of sun slipped beneath the horizon and night's long shadow crept across the capital. A hush spread through the guests as Nanu was introduced to a great roar from the crowd on the island.

Two brilliant cold blue shafts erupted from the tips of the jetties, rising straight up into the sky. Then more bolts burst through the darkness until the entire crescent around the harbor was illuminated by hundreds of glowing columns, giant liquid beams of radiant brilliance impaling the heavens. The guests on the boats emitted a collective "Ahhhhh..." as the streets, the crowds, and, one by one, the majestic stone buildings flashed from darkness.

"Isn't it wonderful?" cried Alius, hugging her brothers.

More food and drinks were passed to the guests, as they marveled at the magical light that flooded the island. "It's miraculous!" cried Demetre, swinging his sister, "Nanu is a genius!"

Simian leaned against the rail absorbing the glorious sight, his bag of books dangling from his shoulder. "Now we can work at night!" he exclaimed quietly.

"Oh, Simian, is that all you ever think about?" scolded his sister, teasing him with those lovely blue eyes. She stood, wrapped an arm around his waist, and pulled him closer with infectious glee.

Her brother turned to gaze in wonder at the reflections skittering across the waves when one of the lights on the jetty flickered, flashed, and vanished...then another and another. Suddenly, there was a rumble from deep inside the mountain, a deep groan rolling over their jubilation like a rogue wave from the molten mantle of the Earth. Demetre pulled away from Alius and screamed to his crew to haul up the anchor and raise the sails.

The calm sea around the beautiful traders roiled with waves rushing from the gap in the jetties as more tremblers thundered beneath the island. The Jasmine listed to starboard and strained to make way as the sails went up and caught a gentle breeze while avoiding the other ships moving in different directions, away from the mouth of the harbor.

As suddenly as they began, the rumbles receded into an unnatural calm and long rolling swells retreated back into the mouth of the jetties. Guests crowded the broad rails on either side of the ship to watch the island slowly shrinking in their wake in stunned silence, broken only by waves slapping the hull and the groan of taut ropes straining against the sails and rigging. Demetre barked orders to his crew, as the Jasmine gained speed and moved to the northeast, away from the harbor and into open waters.

Alius clutched Simian's arm desperately as they both stared back at a stream of tiny figures under burning torches spilling along the jetties and across the bridges from the main island desperate for passage on the armada of vessels spewing from the harbor. Alius looked up at her brother in panic and frustration.

Simian muttered, "It's The Balance! Nanu's disrupted The Balance!"

The men of the crew were hustling around the deck of the ship, tying off lines here and there, straining to harness top speed out of a gentle westerly wind that was driving the trader away from the island.

The side of the conical mountain above the center of the harbor bulged outward and erupted with a great ball of orange flame that blew over the water with a deafening roar, spewing molten rock, searing gases, and clouds of dust and ash thousands of feet into the night sky. Alius and Simian fell to the deck, crushed by the sound, a noise so deep and powerful it wrenched the wind from the lungs.

The Jasmine righted herself as a giant wave broke across the stern and bore the trader on its crest at a pace no ship was designed to carry. The rolling trader tumbled guests across the deck but Alius and Simian landed next to a hatch at the stern, beneath Demetre, who labored to steer the ship with the large tiller. It was a useless struggle, for the ship was carried by the seas, not the wind, but he strained to keep her rudder running with the waves.

Hours later, the ship slowed. An endless train of giant swells carried the battered hull of the Jasmine, her main mast broken and her sails shredded by burning embers falling from the sky. Of the group who gathered to watch the festivities, only twenty-five or thirty remained. The other ships disappeared in the storm and the island, their home, the center of a vast civilization and a culture that touched every corner of the globe, was merely a smoldering ember on the horizon. Over the next few hours, the dark sky blazed with more thundering eruptions until the island vanished into the sea.

Chapter Four

Elsie marched through the door, as George finished the story. Adrian was still seated on the edge of the wing chair, his mouth hanging open in astonishment, a tilted teacup suspended half-way to his lips.

"Now, that's enough history for one day!" scolded Elsie. "The girls are getting ready to go for a swim. Adrian, why don't you run upstairs and put on your swimming trunks?"

George reached to pat Adrian on the shoulder, "We'll talk again soon."

The boy stood to shake George's hand but felt as if his small hand had been grasped in a bear's paw. "Thank you," he stammered, "I'd like that...but how many of the ships survived?"

"No one knows but from what we can deduce, more than a few. We might guess that the work that Simian and his colleagues were carrying ended up in Central and South America, England, and Rome, perhaps? Certainly Egypt, Greece, what was Babylon, India, and China...all of those places where societies suddenly matured and raced ahead of their contemporaries."

Adrian wandered slowly into the foyer, grabbed an *orb*, and climbed the stairs, his mind fumbling to make sense of the strange tale. He found his swimming suit in a drawer in the little chest and put it on. Perched on the edge of his bed, he wondered whether the legends were real, against all logic, or was George just telling stories?

The girls burst into his room. "Come on, let's go!" cried Molly, dragging him into the dark hallway.

They ran downstairs, dropped two *orbs* in the carrier, and turned into the kitchen. Aunt Elsie closed the lid on a small basket of snacks and herded them out the south door, "Dad needs the trolley, so we'll take the wagon," she said.

It was a warm and perfect early summer day as they walked to the old gray barn, where another strange vehicle resided. It was more like a cart than a car and it too seemed to lack any space for an engine. Elsie hopped onto the bench seat and took the wheel. She pushed a round wooden knob on the dashboard and, without a sound, the small wagon began to vibrate gently. "I wish your father would fix that rattle, it shouldn't feel like that!" said Elsie as she eased the truck through a small herd of cows, goats, geese, and chickens onto a cart path to the south.

The girls giggled and Megan leaned over to whisper in Adrian's ear, "Mom's not the best driver in the family and she doesn't like mechanical things. She thinks they should just work perfectly all the time and she gets exasperated when they don't!"

Adrian was still mesmerized by George's story. He turned to Megan and asked, "Is it all true...Atlantis, I mean?"

Megan grinned, "Yes, but that's only as far back as the first coordinated system recorded in the first books. We believe that the first colonies of humans were using the powers, so there's lots more history before that."

"The original garden could have grown around a Positive Crystal," added Molly.

"And maybe a negative one too," said Megan.

After a long, bumpy ride on the cart path, the wagon eased to a stop at the top of a cliff that dropped to the ocean. A stone stairway cut down through the rocks to a crescent of sandy beach at the bottom. The girls raced down the stairs, two at a time. Adrian scanned the children scattered across the shore...some in the water, some building sand castles, a few playing with a ball that occasionally bounced away into the surf. He took the basket from Elsie, offered his hand as support, and followed the girls down to the beach.

Molly ran up to Adrian and took his free hand, "Come along, I want to introduce you."

Elsie retrieved the basket and walked over to a cluster of

brightly colored umbrellas, where a group of women sat talking in the shade.

Molly led her cousin to a small cluster of children. "This is our cousin, Adrian, I'm sure you all heard he was coming to visit for the summer," she said to everyone and no one in particular.

A tall slender boy extended his hand, "Ian. So you're Sara's son, which means I'm your second cousin." He turned to a little blond girl, with sparkling brown eyes and an incredible smile, "This is my sister, Kelly."

The girl beamed, "I'm your cousin too!"

Next was Joshua, about Adrian's age, tall and muscular, with very straight, jet-black hair. His bangs fell over intense dark eyes, probing the new boy, but he smiled and said, "Welcome to Morgan's Knot!"

Megan introduced a tall girl, with long brown ringlets past her shoulders and soft hypnotizing green eyes, as Morgan. He noticed that she bowed slightly, as if she was looking up at him. "I'm pleased to meet you," she said quietly and shook his hand. Her touch was warm but her grip was strong. Calluses on long graceful fingers suggested that she worked with her hands.

He felt his cheeks blush. She was very pretty and he hoped for a chance to know her better.

Megan and Molly introduced him to several other children and then decided that everyone should go for a swim. They ran into the cold water, squeals and laughter scattering a flurry of gulls and sand pipers.

Adrian swam out through the breakers to calmer water. It felt good to stretch his body out, to use his muscles. His brain was still overloaded with George's stories this morning and the daunting reality of his parents' departure. He swam over to the other children who were riding breakers into the beach and caught a wave, racing into shallow water, but the momentum carried him crashing into Morgan. They tumbled in the surf and crumpled onto the sand just at the water's edge.

Adrian rolled over, afraid that he might have injured her, but she was laughing hysterically. He rolled back onto the sand, stood, and reached out to help her up, "Are you alright?"

"Oh, yes," she said, smiling and squeezing his hand as they ran past the breakers to float in the rolling swells.

"When did you arrive?" she asked.

"Yesterday," said Adrian. "My parents are moving our boat to Vancouver, so I get to stay on the island until they're settled."

"Well, I'm glad you're here."

"I think I am too."

Adrian gazed out across the waves and noticed a pair of sharp fins racing through the water. He grabbed Morgan's hand and pointed, "Are those sharks?" He started stroking towards the shore but she just laughed, "No, they're dolphins. They're our friends. Stay where you are." She swam to the nearest fin, which now seemed larger and darker, and the snout of a dolphin rose above the surface with a loud clicking. It almost looked as if it was smiling.

"Oh Dusty, it's nice to see you," said Morgan as she rubbed under his chin and swam behind the dolphin to grab onto his dorsal fin. The dolphin pulled her along to Adrian. Another dolphin surfaced right next to him and he grabbed onto the fin as it darted through the water...faster and faster.

"That's Spot. See the spot on the top of his head?" called Morgan.

The dolphins pulled them back and forth through the surf along the beach. They laughed and screamed as their rides ducked under the surface, only to burst into the air again, until the other children swam out demanding turns riding through the breakers.

Adrian looked over to Morgan, as they treaded water, "That was so much fun! Do they come in often?"

"Oh, yes. I think they enjoy playing with us as much as we like them."

A small herd of mothers wandered down to the edge of the water and called everyone in for a snack. Reluctantly, the children filed up the beach to the umbrellas. Elsie introduced Adrian to the women, "This is Mildred Muldrow, and George's sister, Sheridan Keelty, Robin Green, and Nancy Smith."

Adrian shook hands with each of the ladies, trying to keep their names straight. He guessed that Mrs. Keelty was some sort of distant aunt but he was sure that Elsie would inform him of the family tie. The children sat in a circle at the edge of the shade, eagerly eating sandwiches and fruit passed on small woven platters. Adrian sat between Joshua and Morgan, who asked about his school and the friends he left behind.

"Will you be joining us in class?" asked Morgan.

"I don't know. Nobody's said anything about it." said Adrian. "Do you go to school all year?"

"Oh, yes...but in the summer we don't have to sit in the classroom. We get to go out and see how the things we're learning are actually used in real life. Tomorrow night we get to go to the observatory with Professor Ponte. You'll want to come to that!"

"He's brilliant," said Joshua, "but he's crazy!"

"No, he's not! He's a genius!" replied Morgan emphatically. "He's just…different."

They both laughed and Adrian conjured a fantastical portrait of the Professor, deciding that his first astronomy class might prove entertaining.

After lunch, the children swam and played on the beach with a sphere they called the crazy ball because when one of the children threw or kicked it, it would fly in one direction only to veer off at on odd angle, usually aiming at someone who was not prepared to catch it.

Morgan threw it to Joshua but, in mid-flight, it picked out Adrian and slammed into his face. He fell over backwards and the other children doubled over in laughter. Embarrassed but not hurt, Adrian jumped up, grabbed the ball, and kicked it back into the crowd. It flew towards Ian but took a right angle and headed for little Kelly, who caught it with both hands and smiled that brilliant smile.

As the sun began to dip towards to west, the mothers gathered the children and began to move to the stairs that wound up the face of the cliff. "Come along children," said Elsie. "You have chores to do."

An enormous excavator inched along heavy tracks, clawing through the ancient volcanic mountain beneath clouds of grit glimmering like foul fairy dust in the dim purple glow cast by black *orbs* hanging from the ceiling of the shallow channel. Black diamond teeth pulverized the dense rock and a conveyor ferried the residue to the back of the machine, where it dumped into carts that were heaved down the tunnel by very large men laboring near the frigid depths of the Black Crystal.

"We've waited generations for this!" exclaimed Mandor to no one in particular. In spite of the permanent scowl that creased his rugged face, the promise of this mission made his blazing brooding eyes sparkle beneath long snow-white hair hanging straight and damp. Like all the other workers in the complex, he was dressed in a black leather uniform that glistened with crystalline particles that encrusted everything in the dank atmosphere. "Keep those carts moving!" he roared.

Nanchez lumbered along the track from the far end of the tunnel. "I need three men to work The Crystal and crew the trawler to the mainland," he shouted. The giant's mane of white hair framed knowing eyes in a weathered face that was both pallid and intimidating.

"Take those three I just sent out, they're of no use to me. They move too slowly!"

Nanchez trudged back to the mouth of the tunnel and escorted the men along another colossal corridor through the mechanical wing, the walkway flanked on either side by large black machines that hummed a deep dissonant chorus. The men followed the Keeper through a lock, guarded by two women in black uniforms armed with seeker sticks that could bring a strong man to his knees with the slightest touch, and into a dark tunnel which terminated in a small cavern.

An etched dragon, slithering across the smooth surface of two very large metallic doors, reflected the magenta sparkle of the *orbs*. Nanchez brushed the other men back from the entrance and produced a silver key with a hollow triangle where the teeth might have been. He inserted it in a slot in the left door, releasing the massive metal slabs to swing open with a heavy groan, and stepped back to shove the workers to the entry. The conscripts, too terrified to pass beyond the threshold, cowered on the floor.

"Come on, follow my orders exactly and you might live, now let's get moving!" shouted the huge man, as he placed a slender chain with a black diamond around the first man's neck and shoved him into the chamber.

The first man fell to his knees in fear and awe, for it was common knowledge that the powers within this room were so great that men died just standing before The Crystal. A faceted black gemstone rose stories into the cavern, rotating at an incredible speed and suspended on some invisible finite point a foot above the floor. Its shiny surfaces reflected flashes from *orbs* floating in the corners of the cave. Streaks of purple rippled after a brisk wind that raged around the chamber with a high-pitched whine that rendered talking in normal tones impossible.

"Do not approach The Crystal until you are instructed to do so!" bellowed the giant. "Bring one of those carts!"

The tallest walked over and dragged a small cart back to the base of The Crystal. Nanchez handed a small broom and a metallic scoop to each of them. Although these men were large and muscular, his size was daunting and, as Keeper of the Powers, his status granted absolute authority.

"Now, on hands and knees, crawl beneath the stone and collect the chafe. Deposit all that you gather in these containers on the carts. I'll tell you when to stop!"

The men began sweeping up piles of residue on the smooth surface beneath the whirling stone. The black gems reflected the crazy swirling brilliance around the chamber, fractured glass chasing light through the darkness. The man in the middle reached out and grabbed a black crystal noticeably larger than the sparkling grains accumulated in dazzling dunes sparkling across the floor. He held it up to the light, awed by the color and radiance.

"Give me that!" shouted Nanchez, snatching the jewel from the man's hand. "That is a perfect black diamond," he thought, as he stuffed it into the pocket of his leather uniform. The Masters would be pleased when he delivered a polished stone to them personally.

The men loaded the carts with all the gemstones they could collect from beneath the spinning Crystal and rolled them out into the corridor. Nanchez turned for a last glimpse of the enormous rock. Through all his years as Keeper of The Powers, he still felt awed by the eternal energy and hypnotic beauty. He closed the door and inserted his triangular key to lock it.

The *seer* confirmed the results through each phase of his research with new insights from the Book. If they could control both the Positive and Negative Crystals, they would command all of the power on the island and could begin to extend that control to harness vectors across the rest of the planet.

The tunnel would provide access to a third balancing crystal that regulated the equilibrium between the two primary Crystals. Gain control of that gem and a knowledgeable Keeper could combine the energies of the other two. There was no need for invasion. Those fools on the other side of the mountain lacked a *seer* of their own to devise a defense of their precious Balance. Turn off the power and they would have no option but to capitulate.

Certainly, the giant would relish fulfilling his duties but the science of it, untangling the mysteries of the powers and the vectors was far more intriguing than satisfying the whims of tyrants. He mused to himself, "Wars always provide the need and the motivation for scientific advances."

"Let's go!" he yelled to the three men, who cowered, feeling fortunate to have survived their first encounter with The Black Crystal. They muscled the heavy carts through the tunnels to the entrance and the docks beyond, where the contents would be sorted and packed inside a smooth metal room with sensors capable of detecting the escape of even the tiniest grain.

Sealed metal cases of diamonds were loaded onto a trawler and moved to the mainland. After several transfers, they would be deposited with a personal trader in Amsterdam and sold in small quantities. The proceeds would bolster the Council's already bulging accounts.

Chapter Five

"You'll want a sweater or a jacket," said Megan, as they gathered in the hallway. "The Professor keeps the observatory cold!"

Adrian grabbed a coat from his room and followed the girls down the stairs and out through the front door. The evening was cool and Adrian slipped on his windbreaker.

George pulled up in the trolley and they set off along the path to the mountain, looming like a black hole on the horizon. It was very dark, as the moon had yet to rise above the horizon, and the sky was ablaze with stars, crisp and brilliant.

After a long bumpy ride, they pulled to a stop at the base of the rock column that Adrian noticed standing alone in the barren plain. It rose like a crooked finger pointing into the night and he spied a crescent of light gleaming from the top of the spire.

A stone house nestled into the base of the pillar with two *orbs* suspended next to large wooden doors, which opened with a warm inviting glow as they approached. A very short, chubby man stood silhouetted in the light, called, "Come in, come in, we've been waiting for you."

"Professor, this is my cousin, Adrian," said Molly, as the climbed the steps.

"I'm very pleased to meet you," said the Professor, holding out a small fat hand to pump Adrian's enthusiastically. He was shiny bald on top, with a crazy mane of salt and pepper hair sprouting from around his ears across the back of his head. Tiny spectacles did not quite cover rather large shining eyes under bushy eyebrows attempting to make up for the lack of hair on the top of his head. His lips were full and ready to break into a smile at every moment and he was dressed rather formally with a deep blue waistcoat and a bow tie. He pulled his guest into the room and the door closed behind them.

In the first instant Adrian turned into the parlor, he realized that this space was every kid's fantasy. There were microscopes, telescopes, a model of the solar system made of tiny *orbs* floating and rotating in midair, tangles of wire erupted from boxes covered with dials and switches, two large hawks and an eagle in cages, venomous snakes in glass enclosures, and a skeleton of a human standing in one corner, moving with a rhythm that made it appear to dance to some silent rumba.

Bookcases climbed two stories up every wall, overflowing with well-worn volumes that appeared old enough to have been handed down through generations. Plush, though aging, furniture was arranged in a circle around the room, before a smoldering fire that flickered in a hearth on the far wall, and the whole room glowed. There were no lamps on the tables or *orbs* hanging from the walls, but the high ceiling reflected the entire night sky, radiating the light of the heavens.

Adrian shivered as he scanned the room, settling on the largest black and white cat that he had ever seen. It was sitting on the back of a plum colored sofa, staring intently. Professor Ponte rubbed his plump hand up and down Adrian's back, "The telescope wants to be cold but you'll get used to it. And that is Tic the cat. There used to be a Tac and a Toe but they died when they were very young. You'll have to excuse my rather warped sense of humor!"

Adrian walked over to pet the cat, which stood up and nestled against his stomach. "Welcome," said Tic, looking up at him with a curious stare. "So, you're Sara's son. Interesting."

Adrian's mouth fell open as his hand came to rest in mid-stroke along the hump of the cat's back. He looked to the Professor, who was laughing. "Don't you think that it's a bit arrogant of us to believe that we are the only creatures on the face of the planet who can communicate with each other?"

"Yes, but...?" stammered Adrian. Tic settled back on his perch and closed his eyes. "Why do you keep the birds and the snakes in these cages?"

"Well, each of the birds has suffered an injury. One of the hawks broke a talon and the other hurt his wing. I'm afraid the eagle wandered near hunters on the north side of the island or the mainland and someone must have taken a shot at him. They're all mending nicely. The snakes have volunteered to help with a research project. I'm interested in their ability to sense changes in temperature and vibrations, precisely and instantaneously, before they strike…and besides, we can't have venomous snakes slithering about the house. They'll all be turned out shortly."

"Come along children, your classmates are waiting for us upstairs," said Professor Ponte, with the crook of a finger. He waddled through the dining room to a hallway at the back where a pair of intricately carved doors opened to reveal a tiny elevator. "Come along, come along."

The ornate doors slid closed and the small car rose with astonishing speed. With the ding of a tiny bell, it stopped with a slight bump and the doors opened into a huge dome. An enormous telescope, commanding the center of the room, looked out through an open slot in the curved ceiling.

A group of twelve or fifteen children were gathered around the eyepiece and a tall, slender woman paused her lecture at the interruption. "Oh, here they are!" she cried, with a wide smile that revealed a perfect row of very small teeth.

It took a moment for Adrian's eyes to adjust to the amber glow cast by small *orbs* arranged around the perimeter of the room near the floor, he recognized Morgan, Ian, and Joshua from the beach.

Professor Ponte led the new arrivals across the room, "M'dear, this is Adrian, Sara's son. Adrian, this is my wife, Ester." As they shook hands, Adrian conjured a picture in his mind of an old spinster…she was tall and thin, her gray hair tied in a tight bun at the back of her head, and small eyes peered down at him through dark-rimmed glasses that seemed too large for her face, as if she was gauging his intelligence or his spirit, perhaps. She wore a loose black dress that flowed to the floor and barely concealed her bare feet.

"We're so glad you're here," she said with a smile that stretched thin lips tightly over her too small teeth. He felt that smiling was not a natural response. "Well, gather 'round. We'll be looking at Mars first."

"Ah, Mars," cried Professor Ponte, "reputed to be the God of War, the male planet, and Earth's twin, even though it's only about two-thirds the mass of our planet. Man has always imagined that life existed on the red planet and there is some evidence that suggests that rocks cast off in a cataclysm on Mars eons ago may well have seeded life on Earth."

He stepped to the telescope, "As you look through the eyepiece, notice that there are dark streaks running at angles across the surface of the planet. When they were first viewed and catalogued, it was assumed that these were canals made by intelligent, civilized, and sophisticated cultures but satellite reconnaissance revealed them to be natural structures including a great gorge, far deeper than the Grand Canyon, that scars the surface for hundreds of miles. Those pictures received back on earth also revealed fissures that could only been produced by running water and water is the basis for life as we know it.

Is there life on Mars? Perhaps, but not life as we might hope. I, personally, think there are two possibilities. First, that microscopic life might well live just under the surface of the planet, protected from the harsh environment and the ultraviolet rays of the sun. The planet has a very thin atmosphere that contains little oxygen, which we know to be one of the primary building blocks for life.

The second or additional hypothesis might be that, if intelligent life on Mars survived the process that caused the atmosphere and surface water to evaporate into space eons ago, then it must exist in an underground labyrinth."

"There are plenty of examples of life existing in harsh environments here on Earth. Microbes live in volcanic vents in the ocean, which are high in sulfur dioxide and other harsh toxins that would certainly kill us in short order. Bacteria lives, just under the surface, in places like Death Valley. These life forms transform highly volatile and toxic chemicals into useful ingredients that nourish their very existence and ours too. Life is tenacious. It will happen wherever it is given even the slightest opportunity and I see no reason why organisms might not have adapted to the conditions that exist on Mars today. Unfortunately, we have no direct evidence of little green men, so we must satisfy our creative imaginations with theories.

Also, please notice the lighter...almost white cap that covers the south pole of the planet. It's winter in the southern hemisphere and there's water ice hiding just beneath the carbon dioxide ice that we are seeing on the surface. If there's water, there's oxygen. As the southern hemisphere moves into summer, the cap recedes and disappears, which leads us to the question of where does the moisture go? Does it melt to retreat beneath the surface or does it evaporate into the atmosphere? And, if it does evaporate, where does the moisture come from to form the cap during the next winter? Any ideas?"

Adrian raised his hand. "Couldn't it be a combination of both?"

"Right you are!" cried the Professor with a broad smile. "It seems logical that there is some system, which we do not yet understand, providing for the replenishment of the moisture. Perhaps there are reservoirs and streams running beneath the surface carrying water to soft spots or vents where it can bubble up. And, obviously, great quantities must evaporate.

This leads us to the realization that, if man is to explore our sister planet, we'll need access to liquid water. We all need water in copious amounts for our survival but future visitors will have to process it into oxygen and hydrogen, which can be used to fulfill our need for oxygen and power and to make fuels for the return trip. Unfortunately, water is far too heavy to transport from here to there, so the first explorers will have to find enough water ice to provide for all of those needs."

"Professor, do you think that there are Crystals there? Are there special places like this on Mars?" asked Morgan, her voice echoed softly around the dome.

"It wouldn't surprise me," responded the professor. "There are many of these magical places here on earth and we have no reason to believe that these forces do not exist on other planets."

"Now, we're going to look back through time. M'dear, would you reset the instrument?"

Ester walked across the room to an orange *messenger* suspended in mid-air and spoke softly. The huge telescope began to move, very slowly, and spun around to point almost straight up into the dark sky.

"Are you all aware that light travels at 186,000 miles per second?"

"Yes," replied the group, almost in unison.

"Then does it stand to reason that the farther out into space we look, the farther back in time we are seeing? The light from very distant objects has been traveling for millennia to reach us, so what we are viewing through the telescope happened a very long time ago. The stars and galaxies, that we see, are not really there. They were there when the light started its journey but they moved through space as time passed. The entire universe is expanding at an astounding rate and every galaxy is moving away from its neighbors. In several billion years, the night sky will truly be dark."

The group nodded, understanding if not comprehending.

"Alright, everyone, let's take turns looking through the eyepiece here. What you are seeing is a small section of a large and very young and disorganized galaxy. At the outer edge of the frame, please notice a small intense star surrounded by a dusty disk with two large blobs that can be seen in the curve of darkness just to the right of the star."

Adrian stepped up to the eyepiece and, after a moment, his eye adjusted to the dim specks of light visible through the telescope. Just as the Professor instructed, at the right edge of the galaxy, there was a small bright star surrounded by a thin glowing cloud that formed a disk. About halfway out to the edge of the disk, he could see two murky forms that glowed gently in comparison with the brilliant light of the star. He turned to the Professor, "What are we seeing?"

"Ah, The Question. We're looking at ourselves. That is the Milky Way Galaxy and the star that you are seeing is our sun, billions of years ago. When the light started on it's journey, we were there in space but now we are here and, through some rather intricate properties that bend the path of light as it travels through space and a quirk in the crystals from which the lenses in this telescope were made, we can look back at the birth of our solar system.

The point of this observation is that we're all made of stardust. Everything is made of stardust. Stars go through a lifecycle, just like each of us. They are born when heat and pressure spark a super-dense cloud of hydrogen to condense into thermal life and, by the time they die in a cataclysmic explosion, they have transformed that hydrogen into most of the heavy elements. The remnants hurl through the universe, only to be captured by the gravity of another star that is forming out of a disk of dust that will eventually become a solar system, just like ours. On one of those planets, an atmosphere will develop and, with the help of occasional collisions with passing comets, which are primarily water, and the gases spewed from the molten core through volcanoes all over the planet, rain will begin to fall out of noxious clouds, forming puddles that trickle into streams, that grow to become mighty rivers, that flow into a sea…and it is in the sea that life has the greatest opportunity to ignite."

He paused, grinning, "The stuff that comprised the very first protein, when it transformed from a soup of primordial molecules into a tiny living organism, was made of atoms cast off by that original exploding star. If you take the long view of this hypothesis, each star is made from bits and pieces of a previous star which was made of another…going back until the very beginning, when the first elemental essence exploded to start the universe off with a bang.

As far as we know, admitting that our knowledge is somewhat limited by the vastness of space, there was nothing in this universe before that, so, everything in the universe is made up from the very stuff of that first eruption." He paused and grinned, "If you could collect everything in the cosmos and weigh it, then cast it off again for another billion years and weigh it again, there would be no more or less than when you started. It is finite and we, each of us, is made of those original atoms...stardust."

The discussion continued for two hours, until Ester made a rough coughing noise that erupted from someplace in the depths of her throat, "You've held these children long enough, Ponte. It's time to call it a night."

As the other children began to descend from the tower in groups in the elevator, Adrian turned to the Professor and asked, "You mentioned crystals earlier. What were you talking about?"

"I take it that you've had a chance to explain some of this to him?" asked the Professor of George, who had been standing in the shadows.

"Well, some of it," said George, laughing. "Unfortunately, Elsie decided that swimming was more important!"

"Alright. Let's go down to the parlor, where it's a little warmer, and I'll tell you a bit more." The Professor escorted them to the elevator and, again, the little cab moved at warp speed, only to stop suddenly with a little bump.

Ester scolded the Professor, "You must fix that!"

"Yes, dear," replied the Professor with a wink. "Please, come and sit down."

The remnants of a fire sputtered in the hearth but the library seemed warmer than the observatory. Adrian gazed around the room with the curious glee of a small child in a toy store and finally focused on the caged birds, who were peering curiously at the new boy. He settled on the coach next to Tic the cat, who raised his head and said, "Oh, it's you again," and settled back on his paws and went back to sleep.

The Professor stood before the smoldering ashes in the

fireplace in a doomed attempt to warm his hands behind his back as he rocked from one foot to the other. The smile on his face hinted his delight in telling this story.

"The Crystal," he began and then fell silent for a moment. "There are places all across the Earth that harbor powers that are not utilized in the real world. This is one of those places. Our power source is a very large crystal that transforms static energy from the earth...magnetic, electrical, and chemical...into usable power.

At these points on our planet, those who understand the physical properties of these gems can harvest that energy and use it for positive purposes. I say that with a little bit of reservation, because...just as in physics, for every action, there is a reaction, for every positive, there is a negative, and the same is true of The Crystals. For every stone that gives off positive energy, there is an equal and opposite gem that produces negative energy. We know this to be true on this island. Buried deep inside the mountain, there is another Crystal in perfect balance with our Crystal.

Our ancestors realized that invisible vectors, emanating from the Crystal, like curving, gyrating spokes of a wheel, merged at certain points where the power manifested itself in useful ways. For example, land that grows crops in astonishingly short periods of time, The House of the Four Seasons being my favorite example, but also, giving off intense heat, or waters with amazing healing powers, and there are many others.

Nikola Tesla was very close to discovering the secret but his focus on electrical power blinded him to the combination of energies that allow the vectors to rise from the earth and flow through the atmosphere. There is also the technical problem of tapping into that system in safe and useful ways.

Our vehicles travel along what might be compared to magnetic lines. They do not require an engine, they simply need the opposing force to propel the vehicle along one course and reversing that energy state will drive them back in the other direction.

The same is true for communications, the force fields are already there, all we have to do is tap into them to send pictures or voices or data from one place to another. Obviously, this doesn't mesh with the communication systems throughout the rest of the world, so we have several satellite dishes to send and receive information and to pick up television and telephone signals. To the rest of the world, our signals seem quite normal.

As George might have told you, everyone on the island has had a traditional education. We go to university on the mainland to learn the latest technologies and then adapt them to the powers that exist here on the island. This process has been followed for generations, providing eager, well-educated innovators to push our own developments in new directions."

"You said that there was another Crystal on the island. How do you control it?" asked Adrian.

"Well, we don't." replied the Professor. "You've told him about the others, George?"

"Yes, we touched on it," replied George, who was settled comfortably into a large soft chair, poking at the fire with what appeared to be a broken pool cue. Molly and Megan were lounging on the padded arms, having heard this tale many times before.

"Those families, who were banished from this side of the island, learned to control the powers of the other Crystal, which is reputed to be black. In the same way that our Crystal produces overlapping seasons, The Black Crystal creates an environment that is only winter. No sun reaches the other side of the mountain, except near the summer solstice, so very little grows there. We honestly don't know what foods the others produce without direct sunshine."

"Whatever the forces, the others have learned to harness its powers and to use them for their own benefit. As long as the balance is maintained between the two Crystals, we have no objection to their presence...but one might guess that Black Crystals have been found before. Just as some societies pushed ahead of their times, others have gone the other way. Hitler's Germany is a prime example. Recent atrocities in Africa, The Balkans, and the Middle East and so many other places across the planet are stark testament. We believe that those dark periods of history were manipulated by people who used the powers of the Dark Crystals."

"How did you learn to harness this power?" asked Adrian.

"George told you about Simian the scribe? Yes, well...the reason that he was chosen as a scribe was because he was a *seer*...someone who could read and interpret the writings of the Book of Wisdom's. *Seers* are very rare. They don't appear in every generation. In fact, we are without a *seer* at the moment. Paul, your grandfather, disappeared when your mother was very young and old Justin, who was your great uncle, died several years ago and we have yet to find someone to replace his talents.

Both males and females can be *seers* but the trait seems to be passed through the female child to her children, although we do not have enough information about any other *seers* to verify that conclusion. I would also hazard a guess that there are many people out in the real world who possess these talents but never have any opportunity to understand them or their potential.

Unfortunately, The Book of Wisdoms is not a book that can be translated. In some ways, it's like a computer that you might have used, in that it responds to questions or problems or instructions under rather strict conventions. It's not static like a book with words on paper, rather, it is constantly changing, without beginning or end. Try as I might, I could never understand the writings and had to pose questions to Justin or Paul, who'd seek the answers in the Texts and then instruct me on what they'd found. I always felt it was science by remote control.

All of which leads me to the assumption that the web of vectors and Crystals is, most certainly, a living organism dedicated to maintaining the balance between Mother Earth and those who populate her environment."

Ester made that funny sound in her throat and the Professor looked up. "It's getting late, Dear, we should let these children go home to bed. Besides, we've a full night of viewing ahead of us."

"Right you are, then," replied the Professor with the slightest hint of regret. Adrian had no doubt that he cherished the occasion of telling these tales.

George stood, hugged Ester, and led the girls out the door into the cool night. Adrian turned to the Professor and said, "Thank you for including me. All of this is fascinating. May I come to visit you again?"

"Certainly, my boy, we'll be having another class next week and I do hope that you'll attend." He patted Adrian's shoulder gently, his eyes crinkled and smiled through his tiny glasses.

Chapter Six

Adrian hugged his teddy bear, lying on his bed, staring around the darkened room, haunted by curtains billowing like ghosts in the moonlight. His mind was spinning with all that he learned in the past few days. It was all so strange and, yet, he had no doubt that George and the Professor were telling the truth. Life was different here…magical, but it was all so alien to everything he knew that he found it disturbing…and, perhaps, that was it, everyone seemed to take these magical powers for granted.

There had been no time to miss his parents but, at this moment, he felt homesick just to hear their voices. After what seemed hours of flashbacks to the little house by the bay and a hazy apprehension of their new life in Vancouver, he fell into a fitful sleep and awoke early the next morning feeling anxious and exhausted. He pulled on his clothes and wandered down to the kitchen where he found George sitting at the large table carving up an oversized orange.

Elsie was busy at the stove preparing breakfast. "Good morning, dear," she said brightly. "How did you sleep?"

"Not very well," replied Adrian, rubbing the sleep from his eyes. He sat across from George, as Elsie poured him a glass of juice.

"You've been through a lot in the past few days, there's no doubt," said George kindly. "Would you like to speak with your parents? Might be our last chance before they begin their journey."

"Could I?" asked Adrian, a surge charged through his body.

"Certainly, dear," said Elsie, "We'll ring them up after breakfast."

The boy was suddenly hungry and ate everything that Elsie put before him. Presently, the girls appeared in their pajamas, barely awake and annoyed with the transition. Molly hugged an old doll with bright red hair, which she plopped into Adrian's lap as she plunked down next to him. "That's Martina, be nice to her," she moaned.

"Where'd she get that name?" asked Adrian with a smirk, looking at the doll whose eyelids opened and closed as you moved her up and down. The left lid was jammed partially open, as if she was half asleep, not unlike his cousin.

"It's just a name that I found in a story, so that's what I call her!" whined Molly, impatiently. Elsie brought two more plates to the table and the girls picked at their eggs, fish, and fruit. Adrian was still hungry so he grabbed another muffin from the basket in the center of the table, stuffed it in his mouth to silence an anxious tongue, deciding that perhaps this was not the moment to be teasing his cousin.

George led his nephew into the study where a large *messenger* sat on a credenza behind the desk, "Sit right here at the desk and turn around to face the *messenger*. Now say your telephone number out loud. We won't be able to see them but we'll hear them, just like a normal telephone."

Adrian rattled off his telephone number, thinking of the little blue house by the bay and the sound of the telephone ringing in the kitchen. He missed his home.

"Hello," said his mother's voice at the other end of the line.

"Mom, it's Adrian!"

George chuckled, "You can speak in normal tones and she'll hear you just fine."

"Oh, I've been wanting to hear your voice. How are you, how do you like the island?"

"It's as magical as you said it would be and I've been having fun with Molly & Megan. George and Elsie are excellent and I got to go to an astronomy class with Professor Ponte last night. That was really interesting."

His mother paused, "I'm sure that you're learning things you never imagined. I'm sorry I didn't prepare you for all of this but there really isn't any way of explaining it unless you're there. I'm so happy that you're having a good time."

"When do you leave?" asked Adrian.

"We hope to put out to sea tomorrow. We've sold the house and the movers are here moving things into a large truck in the driveway. It's kind of sad but we're both excited about our new life and we can't wait to see you."

"Me too," said Adrian, suddenly sad, knowing that it would be more than two months before he saw his parents again. "I miss you."

"I miss you too and I'm hoping for favorable winds so we can accomplish everything as fast as possible. Promise! Here comes Dad. Would you like to talk with him?"

"Yes," replied Adrian, "but I don't want to stop talking to you."

"I know, me too. I love you Adrian and I miss you. You be good for Elsie and George and have a great time. We'll be in touch as soon as we get to Vancouver."

Sara handed the phone to John, wiping tears from her eyes, turned out the back door, and sat on the step next to her blooming rose bushes for a little cry on her own.

"Hey fella, how are you?" asked John.

"I'm fine. The girls are fun and Elsie and George have been kind. I just wish that I could come with you."

"I know," said his father. "I wish you could too but we think this is the best way to do this and I sure appreciate the fact that you're going along with our decision."

"I don't have much choice, do I?" whispered Adrian, resigned to the verdict.

"You hang in there, son," said John, "and we'll be in touch as soon as we can. I love you."

"I love you too, Dad," replied Adrian. The line went dead.

———————

It was warm and cloudy as John and Sara stowed the last of their provisions into the galley. Sara cast off the lines and The Sparrow drifted away from the dock, turning to the break in the jetties. They waved to the small group of friends who had gathered to see them off and hoisted the sails.

The wind was steady from the northwest, so John set the spinnaker and the beautiful sloop picked up speed, as Sara winched in the slack, heading south.

John returned to the stern and took the helm. Sara wrapped an arm around his waist, "Are you sad?"

"Yes, we built our life together in this little hamlet, but I'm excited too. This trip is going to be an adventure and we haven't had a vacation in a very long time."

"I'm feeling better about Adrian, although I'm feeling a bit guilty about not doing a better job of preparing him for all that he's learning. We know he's safe and he's going to have fun with the girls but I feel as if we're closing the door on one part of our life together. I have to admit that I'm a little bit anxious about opening the door to the next," she said, looking up into his eyes. "I love you."

"Oh, I almost forgot," said John, kissing her tenderly. He reached into his pocket to withdraw a small box, wrapped with red ribbon, "I have something for you."

Sara took the tiny package and removed the lid to find a gold locket on a slender golden chain. She opened the charm to a tiny smiling portrait of Adrian, "Oh, I love it. I'll wear it forever!"

They hugged across the tiller, looking up at the white sails and the red monogram on the spinnaker...a perfect cross, even on each side, surrounded by a slender crescent whose arms enclosed a tiny six-pointed star.

In spite of a mild breeze from the east, the heat and humidity were oppressive as the Sparrow eased into a dock at the far end of the wharf in Montego Bay, away from the gleaming oversized yachts and massive hotels. Sara tossed lines to a dockhand waiting at the end of the wharf.

"My name is Sammy. How can I help you, Mon?" said the small, wiry boy, taking up slack to tie off the ropes to cleats on the edge of the wharf.

"We'll be needing fuel and fresh water," replied John, "And we could stand to re-supply our stores."

"There's a grocery just up the gangway," said Sammy, pointing to a small stall beneath a large white sign with 'FOOD' painted in bold red letters. "I'll take care of the fuel and water for you."

Sara smiled and thanked the boy, as they walked along the old wooden planks to the grocery. They were only gone for twenty minutes, as there was limited choice in the supplies the little store had to offer.

"You're all fixed up, Mon," smiled Sammy.

"We'd like to spend the night. Is there somewhere we can tie up until morning?" asked John.

"Do you have showers on the dock?" added Sara.

"Sure, Mon. You can tie up to that buoy out there and the showers are just up the way, here," he replied, pointing to a red marker floating twenty yards from the dock and then to a small enclosure with a metal roof at the end of the gangway. "I'll get your ticket."

The boy ran up to a shack and returned with a small slip of paper. John paid him, adding a sizable tip.

"I can't wait for a shower!" smiled Sara, gathering clean clothes from a locker.

"I know what you mean. It's been a while!"

"Meet you back here but I won't promise that I'll be quick. I'm going to enjoy this!"

They showered and moved The Sparrow out to the buoy. Sammy followed with a skiff and ferried them back to the dock.

"Are there any good restaurants near by?"

"Sure Mon," laughed the little man, "What kind of food do you want?"

"Anything that hasn't been frozen!" laughed Sara.

"You'll find tourist restaurants all along the quay but there's a lovely little place just up the hill called Mona's. Follow this road up to the second crossing and take a right. It's about two blocks on, Mon."

"Thank you, we'll be back in a little while."

They strode off up the hill and turned to the right, where they found the little restaurant with a crude sign above the door that read "Mona's." It was rather shabby but they were tired and ready for a hearty meal.

Although the café was not elegant, Mona, the proprietress and chef, doted over them, explaining that everything on the menu was grown, raised, or harvested from the sea by her family, and the dinner was truly extraordinary. They shared a leisurely bottle of wine, followed by coffee and a sweet tart with a sugar glazed crust that Mona prepared just for them.

"I feel almost human," smiled Sara, "how about you?"

"I love your cooking but it's been weeks since we had a meal like this and I have to admit that I enjoyed every bite. The breadfruit was perfect with the snapper," said John, leaning back in his chair with a satisfied sigh and a sip of warm coffee.

"I'd love to go shopping in the morning. Do you think that we could spare the time?"

John smiled, "How did I know that you'd want to shop?"

"I haven't the faintest idea," laughed Sara.

They walked arm-in-arm back to the quay to find Sammy sitting at the end of the dock staring up at the stars. He stood to greet them. "I'm sorry, I was just watching Mars, see there, the bright red one. It's as close to Earth as it will be for another two years, so it seems bigger and brighter," he said, pointing about half way up in the sky to the east. "How was your meal?"

"It was marvelous," said Sara, "and Mona is an angel."

"Well, she is my aunt," smiled the slender boy with gleaming perfect teeth. "Can I give you a lift back to The Sparrow for the night?"

John asked, "How did you know that was Mars?"

"I read an article in the London Times. The tourists leave their newspapers in the restaurants and I go by to pick them up everyday to share with my uncle. I read everything."

"I'm impressed," said John.

The next morning, they caught a taxi to the vast open market and found stalls offering an endless variety of native foods, fresh meats and fish, vegetables and fruits in every imaginable color, bouquets of flowers overflowed their containers in one stall where John bought a few passionflowers for Sara. Rich irresistible scents drew them to another stand offering freshly baked pastries. They wandered from one to the next, until they came to a line of stalls selling fabrics in bright garish colors and patterns.

Sara was entranced and pawed through pile after pile until she found a bolt of very sheer cloth, certainly the deepest, most vibrant blue that she had ever seen. She wrapped the fabric around her waist and modeled for John, "Think I could make a new frock out of this?" she laughed.

"It is beautiful. I've never seen any blue that was so intense and it certainly shows off your blond hair and those wonderful eyes. They almost match!"

"Done then," she smiled and turned to the shopkeeper to make her purchase.

"Ah, that is a perfect choice!" said the man behind the sagging table. His weathered skin glistened like polished ebony under a white goatee and little wire-rimmed glasses perched on the end of a broad nose. He peered over his spectacles as he spoke, "It is said that this material was coveted by the kings of old. It is the finest gossamer and as thin as a hummingbird's feather."

"I'd like four yards, please."

The old man measured out the blue cloth with his rough, knobby hands on a well-worn yardstick, tacked to the table. A pendant hung from his neck, swinging back and forth as he worked. Sara could not help but notice that it was exactly the same color as the fabric that she was buying. "I think that you'll want just a bit more. I won't charge you any extra."

"That's a beautiful pendant you're wearing," said Sara.

The old man held it out to her. It was round with a perfect cross in the middle, surrounded by a slender crescent moon, whose points almost touched at the top, restraining a tiny star. The cross and moon were mother of pearl and raised above the vibrant blue translucent background. "It almost matches your eyes," said the old man softly. "It is said that this is the mark of an ancient *seer* named Protus."

"What do you know of *seers*?" asked Sara, struggling to conceal the shock straining to displace the calm, joyous smile on her face.

"It is believed that they could read from the ancient texts."

"That may be but how do you know about *seers*?"

"I know many things about many things." The old man smiled, slyly, "This is a magical island and we believe that the descendants of the ancient *seer*, Protus entrusted the magic to our ancestors, when his people fled to this island to evade the ghost warriors. The legend claims that they gathered the last of their civilization and headed off across the Caribbean to the Pacific, where they found an island that offered a chance to start again. It is called 'La Isla de los Ninos'…The Island of the Children, with hope that future generations might survive to protect the magic."

Sara stared at the old man, gazing at her over his little glasses, waiting, perhaps, to gauge her reaction, but the edges of his lips curled ever so slightly. She felt that he was telling her a secret that he shared with no one else.

He continued, "We all believe that we are somehow related to those people. Most of the people of Jamaica will tell you that they have proof but they're all lying. I am not."

Sara held out the money that she owed the man and he made a point of touching her hand, when he took the bills. She felt an electric tingling in her fingers, where his hand brushed against hers.

"You have a safe journey, pretty lady. You'll find more than you are looking for." He handed her the change and the brown paper package with her fabric. "I will see you again."

Sara's voice trembled, "Thank you." She turned and walked over to John, who was looking at shell trinkets in a stall covered with a yellow tarp. When she looked back, the old man and the fabrics had vanished.

Chapter Seven

Adrian thanked George for letting him use the *messenger* to talk with his parents and wandered upstairs to his room. As he approached the door, it said, "Back so soon?" with a snicker, and creaked open to allow him to enter.

He sat on the edge of his bed pining for his home and his parents. He missed life by the bay, all that he had known as normal, and wondered whether his friends were executing their plans for the summer. He thought about the Sparrow, the feeling as she moved through the waves, the sounds and smells, feeling banished by his parents from their adventure.

Molly knocked on the door, peeking around the edge to say, "Mom was wondering whether you might help us with our chores. The festival is this weekend and she's in a tizzy, wanting to get everything done. You know how mothers are!"

"Of course," sighed Adrian.

The children spent the next days harvesting an amazing variety of vegetables from the gardens, hauling milk from the barn to the cold cellar, and when one chore was finished, Elsie had more demanding discharge in the proper sequence. She anchored herself in the kitchen, cooking and preparing endless dishes, and sent the children off in different directions to collect whatever was required for the next.

Adrian was thankful to be busy. It provided an escape from his memories of home and his anticipation of their new life in Vancouver.

He and Megan were hauling a heavy basket of tomatoes and peppers from the south garden to the kitchen, when a large red Irish setter came bounding up the path. His tail wagged frantically and he smiled up at them. "That's Brandy," said Megan. "He lives down the path at the Keelty's."

Brandy pranced around the children, sniffing at the basket. "I hope you'll have something for me at the party," he said, tilting his head inquisitively, his sad brown eyes peering hopefully at Megan.

Adrian's mouth dropped open.

"I see no reason why you humans should enjoy the best dishes on the island without sharing!" said Brandy, leaning to check the scents on Adrian's pants and shoes.

They put the basket down beneath a large old oak tree and ran their hands over his soft coat as Brandy rubbed against their legs. Adrian sat down in the shade and the red dog crawled into his lap, "You're a little large to be a lapdog, fella."

Brandy licked his face all over and Adrian erupted in giggles, "I just like being with you kids. The grown-ups around here don't spend enough time playing!"

"Well, we'll play with you but you'll have to wait until we finish our chores. Mom's on a rampage to get everything ready for the festival." said Megan, rubbing the dog's soft ears.

"All right, I'll come back later, when you're not so busy, It's the same in every house on the island," sniffed Brandy, as he ran down the path towards the Keelty's.

Adrian and Megan picked up the heavy basket and climbed the steps to the kitchen. "Talking dogs and cats...now that's magical," grinned Adrian.

Megan laughed. "Yes it is magical, when you think about it. We're around the animals all the time, so we don't really appreciate the fact that this probably doesn't happen anywhere else in the world. I'm sure they absorb every word we say but only respond when they want to and I'm afraid I don't understand when they talk to each other."

As they dragged the basket into the kitchen, Adrian thought that the only thing better than having a pet was having a pet who could talk with you. "This is an amazing place."

—————∽∽∽—————

The children loaded basket after basket into the trolley as the sun dipped behind the ridgeline. Upon Elsie's close inspection, it was evident that there was not enough room for all of them, so George brought the wagon around for the children to drive.

Other than Molly saying, "Oh, you are going to like this!" Adrian really had no clue about what to expect at the 'festival' but everyone on the island was invited and there was little doubt that every mother had prepared as much food as his aunt.

They set off along the winding path to the little village by the cove, George and Elsie in the trolley and Molly and Megan taking turns steering the wagon, which veered randomly from side to side along the path.

Adrian leaned between the girls from the back, "I have a question for you two. When we arrived and when my parents left, I noticed that there were no people in the village. Does anyone really live there?"

"No, the village is mostly for show and for distributing supplies when the trawlers return from the mainland. The shops provide a convenient way to store things that people will need, except the pub, which is well stocked and usually busy in the evenings. Occasionally, even though this island is not really on any maps, a boat will stumble on us and pull into the docks. The grown-ups scurry around to make it look like it's inhabited and the people on the boat go away without realizing the ruse," said Megan.

"It's so funny to watch them put on a show. Mom pretends to be the fishmonger's wife and hollers at the men to hurry-scurry. She's hysterical. Other people have different roles, including some of the children...usually whoever's handy."

"We know they're coming because Professor Ponte's instruments are always keeping an eye on the horizon. The Crystal reacts when anything approaches the boundaries of its field."

"So the whole village is just a set, like in the movies?"

"Well, sort of, but there's more to it, as you'll see. Whoever built it, generations ago, must have been a child at heart because the inside is an amusement park."

The village overflowed with people. Vehicles of every description were parked at odd angles here and there and small mobs were carting supplies into the buildings. All the doors were standing open to the evening breeze and warm light spilled out into long shadows.

Molly pulled the wagon up to one of the buildings and slammed on the brake. It lurched and the children burst out laughing. "Maybe you should let me try to drive this thing on the way back! I couldn't do any worse than you!" said Adrian.

They trotted over to the trolley to help carry the baskets into the fish market. Adrian stepped through the door and was totally convinced that he was entering a real fish market. The air was heavy with the odor of the fresh catch listed on the blackboard behind the counter and a few flies buzzed about even though there were no fish in the glass case at the front. He followed the girls through a doorway on the left into an enormous room, behind the facades in front, connecting several buildings together.

Long dining tables lined the center of the room, while tall, deep benches lined the walls to serve the guests. Each table was covered with white linens and huge bouquets of flowers. Elsie instructed the children about where to place each of the baskets, "Deserts over here, vegetables and hors d'ouerves over there." They made several trips back and forth to the trolley before everything was in place.

A raised stage extended from one end of the hall with musical instruments playing softly, although there were no musicians. A violin, a stand-up bass, a flute, several horns, a piano, and, Adrian's favorite, a drum set with sticks bouncing and twirling off drumheads and cymbals.

Molly and Megan led Adrian out through the fish shop and down the quay, past an apothecary and a little pub, to another group of storefronts. They entered through a fishing tackle shop, which offered every variety of fishing lures imaginable. Rods of every length, reels in silver and gold finishes, hooks, sinkers, lines, and bobbers filled the racks. Several bait tanks bubbled against the back wall. Adrian peered into one, as they passed, and noticed that someone had stocked it with goldfish. Except these not the ordinary variety of murky fishbowls, they literally glowed orange like little marine fireflies.

They stepped through the door at the back of the tackle shop into another cavernous room resonating with the noise of children's screams and laughter. A herd of giant colored eggs bobbed a foot above the floor in an endless chain reaction as the youngsters twisted steering levers frantically to ram everyone else, without being bumped in return.

To the right, a carousel rotated slowly, inhabited by all sorts of intricately carved animals...horses, butterflies, dragons, a giant panda that could hold several children in its lap, and a unicorn, certainly the most beautiful creature in all the ancient myths, with a slender golden horn growing from the top of its bowed head. Some of the parents and many of the smaller children floated around and around on the backs of these wonderful creatures beneath small colored *orbs* splattering vibrant traces around the walls and floor.

At the other end of the room Adrian spied something that resembled a roller coaster without wheels. Its cars hovered just above the floor and children and parents were loading in and out. "All aboard!" shouted an older boy.

Molly leaned over and whispered, "That's Patrick, isn't he a dream?" gazing at the boy. Adrian smiled and looked over at Megan, who wore the same lovelorn look.

"Girls!" he cried. "Come on, let's go for a ride!"

He grabbed his cousins and ran to the coaster just in time to climb into the last car. The tram shuddered and began to move just as they settled into their seats. It crashed through a door with a bang and bounced up a staircase into a wonderland populated with animated creatures. Clowns and goblins danced to loud thumping rhythms. Great lions and tigers rushed at the cars before an elephant reared up, screeching, and it seemed that they would certainly crash, until the lead car swung to the right and the elephant to the left at the very last instant. Around and around, up and down at breakneck speed until the train hurtled toward a pair of French doors. The riders screamed with delight as it burst through the frame and twisted around the outside of the building, only to dive back through another window, down a long chute, where it squealed to a stop, ready for the next group of riders.

Molly, Megan, and Adrian doubled over in laughter. "Let's find something a little more gentle," he said, clutching an aching stomach. The girls laughed even harder. Patrick smiled patiently and reached to help the girls out of the car. Molly and Megan blushed.

They walked out a door at the back of the building under the biggest, broadest oak tree that he had ever seen. Hand-in-hand, the three children could not reach even half way around the trunk. Glowing colored disks vibrated between knobby roots twisting along the ground. Megan stepped on one and rose up into the tree, where she stepped off, leaned over a banister on the landing, and shouted, "C'mon!"

Molly and Adrian hopped on the pulsing circles and floated up to meet her. There were rope ladders to climb to the very top of the tree and platforms, like tree houses, scattered in the foliage. Slides zigzagged through the branches and around the trunk and children screamed as they zoomed on the chutes that pointed up or down, allowing the kids to fly along in either direction. The whole tree twittered with the musical glee of children hanging and climbing on every limb within reach.

On the next landing, they found Joshua, Morgan, Ian, and little Kelly. "Isn't it wonderful?" squeaked Kelly.

"Yes, it is." said Adrian, enchanted with her smile.

Joshua patted him on the back and said, "Glad you're here." Adrian grinned and turned to Morgan, who smiled shyly. Although she was taller than Adrian, she bowed her head slightly, creating the impression that she was looking up at him.

"I'm glad to see you again," she said softly. Adrian blushed and moved next to her, where they could watch the children zipping around the tree. Suddenly a hairy red flash zoomed by and Adrian realized it was Brandy, the Irish setter, smiling his biggest smile, his pink tongue flapping out the side of his mouth.

The red dog trotted over a few minutes later, "Why can't I have fun too?"

"I can't really think of any reason why you shouldn't. Is this your favorite part of the festival?"

"Well, they won't let me drive the bumper cars and riding on the backs of carved animals on the carousel seems kind of strange," said Brandy as he sauntered over to one of the colored circles and descended to the ground. "I'll see you in a little while, I smell food!"

The children climbed through every part of the tree until the gong of a large bell summoned all to dinner.

They found an open table at the far end of the room from the bandstand. Parents and children danced in front of the small stage and everyone wandered from one serving table to another filling their plates with an astonishing variety of delicacies. Everything Adrian tasted was delicious and he was sure that no one would leave hungry.

Joshua leaned over to Adrian and asked, "What did you think of the Professor's story about seeing ourselves in the past, the other night? I'm bettin' he was pulling our legs!"

"I don't know," replied Adrian. "I don't see why it's not possible. Who knows where the Earth has been since the light left that star eons ago."

"Ah, you're daft," laughed Joshua. "Light is the fastest thing in the universe and it travels in straight lines, so how could we possibly get ahead of ourselves?"

"You do have a point," mused Adrian, "but I think I'd like to believe that it might be possible. Besides, I read about a theory where large objects bend light in space, so it might have taken the long way around."

Joshua did not appreciate the joke.

The evening continued with music and dancing, and more food and drink. The younger children began to fall asleep on their parent's laps and it was close to midnight by the time Adrian, Molly, and Megan packed the baskets back into the trolley.

"Stay close behind us on the way back, girls." ordered George.

"Can I drive?" asked Adrian.

"Well, I don't see why not. Here climb in and I'll show you. You just push this knob to start her," he said, reaching in to press a knob on the dashboard. Now, you steer with the wheel and use that pedal on the floor. Push it forward, to go forward, and push it back the other way to stop or reverse. Think you can handle it?"

"I think so," said Adrian, climbing behind the wheel. His parents never let him actually drive their car. Once in a while, one or the other would secretly let him sit on their laps and steer along the back roads at home.

George went around to the front of the trolley, climbed in, and slowly pulled away up the hill. Adrian pushed down on the pedal and the wagon lurched forward, much too fast. He released the pressure and it slowed to a stop. "I think this is going to take some practice!" he blushed, pushing more gently on the pedal. Molly and Megan giggled uncontrollably. The wagon started forward again and gained speed. Two *orbs* mounted at the front of the wagon lit the path and Adrian followed the glowing *orbs* on the back of the trolley.

He found steering the wagon was much the same as steering his parent's car but rather than pointing the front into a curve, the wagon seemed to turn from the middle, all of which functioned far more easily when he anticipated where he was steering before he actually reached the bend.

The two vehicles bounced along the paths through darkened fields back to the House of Four Seasons, over the bump at the gate, and around to the kitchen door. They unpacked the baskets and set them on the table in the kitchen. "I'm much too tired to deal with that tonight, just leave them there and I'll look after this in the morning." said Elsie. "It's late and time for you children to be in bed. Give us a hug and off you go."

The children hugged Elsie and George, collected *orbs* from the carrier at the bottom of the stairs, and slowly marched off to bed.

Chapter Eight

Adrian padded down the stairs and found Elsie and George in the kitchen. His uncle was dressed in heavy clothing, despite warm sunshine gleaming through the kitchen window. A yellow slicker was hanging from a hook next to the south door.

"Ah, Good morning," said Elsie with a tired smile. "Did you enjoy the festival?"

"It was wonderful," replied Adrian, rubbing the sleep from his eyes. "The rides, the giant tree, the delicious food, and the fact that everyone gets together to celebrate the beginning of summer. Thank you for including me."

"It was our pleasure."

"How did you like driving the wagon," asked George.

"It took a while to get the feel of it. It doesn't turn like a regular car, it sort of turns in the middle."

George laughed, "Yes, it is rather odd at first, but I think you've got the idea! A little practice and you'll master it."

"Are you going someplace?"

"Yes, today is fishing day, so a group of the men get together to take the trawlers out. We'll be gone until tomorrow."

"That sounds like fun."

"It's hard work and we stay out for twenty-four hours."

"I'd love to go," said Adrian, hoping for another adventure.

"Well, we're pretty well set up for this run but, perhaps, next time."

"Okay," replied Adrian.

George kissed Elsie, grabbed the slicker and a gear bag, and headed out, as Adrian sat down for breakfast. It wasn't long before the girls wandered into the kitchen and plopped down in their chairs.

"Are you two a little bit tired?" asked Elsie.

They both groaned, which was answer enough. Elsie placed their plates on the table and the twins picked at their food.

"Has Daddy left already," asked Megan?

"Yes, a few minutes ago."

"Could we take the wagon to the bluff to watch them go out?" asked Molly.

"Certainly, and, while you're about it, why don't you take Adrian for a tour of the island. I'm sure that he'd love the forest," suggested Elsie.

"Oh, lovely," said the girls together.

Adrian finished his breakfast and excused himself. He wandered into the living room and noticed that slight chill. The north windows shimmered with a thin glazing of frost on the glass. The three portraits on the credenza caught his attention and he stared at the eyes of the two women and then the man, whose gaze seemed vibrant and alive, curious and determined. He sauntered into George's study and noticed golden brown fields to the west.

He met the girls in the foyer and they scrambled upstairs to change their clothes. "You'll love the forest. Promise!" said Molly, suddenly revived. "Let's hurry!"

The children rushed back to the kitchen where Elsie was putting some small bundles of food into a basket, "Here's some food for your lunch and some treats for your friends. How about being back by early afternoon, so we can get the chores finished?"

"We'll be back in plenty of time," said Megan, "and thanks for the food!"

Adrian followed the twins through the kitchen door into a warm, bright summer morning. Two cows, several goats, and a flurry of chickens met them at the barn. "Did you bring us something?" asked one of the goats.

"No, you've already had your breakfast," said Molly. "I know you've been fed!"

"What's in the basket?" asked another.

"Our lunch! Now move out of the way, we're taking the wagon out and we certainly don't want to run over any of you. Besides, Adrian's driving and he's new at this!"

The animals slowly wandered across the path, as the children climbed into the wagon and pulled out of the barn. Adrian felt a bit more confident about his driving skills and the wagon did not jump or buck when he gently applied pressure to the pedal. They turned south on the cart path to the bluff overlooking the crescent beach.

The salt air smelled fresh and clean on a gentle wind from the east and sunlight glistened on the water around the three trawlers just pulling out from the cove under a flock of seagulls, hoping for a midmorning treat. Two of the trawlers turned north while the third pulled out of formation heading south.

"I wonder where they're going?" said Adrian, pointing to the lone boat.

"Oh, they're probably making a run to the mainland for supplies. I'm sure they'll join up with the others later," said Molly.

"Let's go to the forest!" said Megan, charging back to the wagon to follow the path along the coast, then west through fields mature with green growth, meadows of grains, soy, and vegetables of every variety. Here and there, thickets of blackberries beckoned them to sample. Acres of corn and cotton stretched to the south as they turned west to a forest climbing the jagged ridge that meandered along the center of the island.

The children parked the wagon near a track into the forest and pulled the basket from the back. Molly ran up the path and disappeared into the shadows of ancient trees clustered into a dense natural fortress for the wildlife of the island. Megan and Adrian followed but hesitated for a moment to adjust to the darkness.

A voice, from above, chirped, "Did you bring anything for us?"

Adrian looked up at a cardinal, sitting on a limb above their heads, and felt many pairs of eyes staring down from the branches of the nearest trees.

"We'll have to see what's in the basket, when we have our lunch," said Megan. "There might be something left over for all of you!"

The birds screeched in anticipation and fluttered above their heads, guiding the children along a narrow path deeper into the forest until they trundled down a hill to a small brook that flowed cool and clear into a pool. Adrian could see small fish, flitting about beneath the surface. Shafts of light cascaded down through gaps in the thicket of giant trees reaching to block out the sky.

They settled on smooth boulders to rest and to play in the creek. Although he could not see anything or anyone near them, Adrian sensed that they were being watched. Other than the chattering of the birds, the forest was almost silent. He sat down on top of a large rock, as the girls took off their shoes and waded into a shallow pool.

"This is really beautiful."

The two girls smiled mischievously. "Yes, it's one of our favorite places," said Molly, smirking. "It's always full of surprises!"

Before Adrian could react, something hit him hard in the back and he tumbled head first down the face of the rock into the water. He rolled over to find a beautiful doe perched comfortably atop the boulder.

"Oh, Daphne, did you have to do that?" laughed Molly.

"We haven't been introduced. I'm Daphne. Who are you?" asked the doe.

"I'm Adrian. Nice to meet you too!" said Adrian, sitting up to wipe the water from his face. He was completely soaked which was excuse enough for the girls and Daphne to laugh even harder. Adrian could not restrain himself and splashed a wave up at Daphne, who gracefully sidestepped the curtain of droplets.

Adrian looked around and noticed two deer standing behind him. Several raccoons, a few squirrels, chipmunks, and a small bear joined the circle around the boy in the pool and they were all peering down at him. He peeled off his shirt and shoes and pitched them on the shallow bank.

"Just don't foul our water!" exclaimed the little bear.

Adrian stretched out and let the water cover his body. It was refreshingly cool and he was still embarrassed and in no hurry to climb out.

"Adrian is our cousin," said Molly, "so be nice to him!"

All of the animals greeted Adrian, in turn, and the small bear moved to sit on a rock next to him, "I'll bet you never had a conversation with a bear before!"

"That's true," replied Adrian. "I guess I should feel privileged!"

"You should!"

"I always felt sorry for the animals that I've seen in the zoo. It is much nicer meeting you this way."

"I've never been to a zoo but I understand they are rather sad. It's too bad that The Balance doesn't exist everywhere in the world. Man and nature have so much to share, so much to gain from working together, and so little time if they don't," said the small bear.

One of the raccoons climbed into Megan's lap, "If only mankind would understand what they're missing. It would be so much better if all of the animals and all of the humans could sit down and talk with each other."

One of the other raccoons pulled at the cover of the basket. "Hey, you!" yelled Megan, "that's our lunch! We might share some of it with you but you don't get first pickings!"

The raccoon backed out of the basket, a bit ashamed at being caught in his attempted larceny. "I'm hungry too. Let's see what mother made for us!" said Molly, as she crawled over to lift the lid and pull sandwiches and drinks from the basket for Megan and Adrian.

"Oh, look," she said, "Mother has provided for you too!" She pulled some corn, nuts, and leftover cookies from the basket and gave each of the animals something to eat. She spread dried grains and nuts on a flat rock for the birds.

"I'd prefer fish," said the Bear.

"Beggars can't be choosers," said Meg, "perhaps that's why we call you 'Beggar'! Here, have a cookie, I know you like chocolate!"

Beggar took the cookie between his paws and nibbled around the edges, "My compliments to your mother!"

The children played with the menagerie for another hour, before the sun was high overhead, time to head back to the House of the Four Seasons. All of the animals formed a procession to escort the guests to the edge of the forest.

Daphne bumped Adrian in the back again, "I'm sorry that I pushed you into the water."

"Oh, that's alright," said Adrian, wrapping his arms around the doe's neck, "It's been a pleasure meeting all of you!"

Nanchez and Mandor examined the latest calculations on a *messenger* tablet beneath the purple glow of one of the *orbs* in the tunnel. "We're almost through," said Mandor, "perhaps another fifteen or twenty feet at most."

"I agree," said Nanchez, turning to shout, "Stop the machine!" Glittering dust billowed through the cold damp air hanging in tunnel, Mandor coughed, "We need to consult with the Masters before we go any further."

The pale giants trudged down the rails, through the north entrance into the dark shadows cast by the mountain in the late afternoon for a breath of fresh air. The black peak soared into a spectrum of streaming colors splashed across the sky, a good omen. Three giant inverted crescents provided access from the docks to the labyrinth of tunnels that honeycombed the mountain. The entry on the right opened to the mechanical wing, where rows of dark magenta *orbs*, suspended along the passageway descending into the earth, illuminated the cavern with a cold smooth glow. They greeted coworkers with stern nods, passing giant machines, rumbling and groaning in large alcoves carved into the dense rock on either side, and marched through a series of locks to the chambers of the Masters.

They approached two large black metallic doors and were met by a very small woman with dark darting eyes and straight white hair, standing at attention, her seeker stick barring any hope of access to the inner sanctum. The dark *orbs* shimmered on her black leather uniform as she scanned the men and asked, "Are you ready?"

"Yes, we're almost through," replied Mandor. "We need to speak with the Masters."

"They've been anxiously awaiting your success," replied the small woman. "Please come with me." She inserted a small triangular key into a slot and the huge doors swung out, forcing the men to step back.

Only the Masters and their immediate subordinates ventured past this threshold. The men felt privileged and nervous to be delivering their report in chambers. They exchanged a knowing glance as the tiny woman led them into a large round room, rough cut from the black rock. The domed ceiling threatened the uninitiated with terrifying sculptures of dragons, gargoyles, bats, serpents, giant insects and all the other creatures of the night crawling up to the source of a single shaft of dark purple light, illuminating the center of a raised circular slab of stone. Five large men sat on the far side of the circle, wearing the same black leather uniforms as the workers and technicians, but each wore a large black diamond pendant. Nanchez supplied these prize gems as protection against the forces emitted by the Black Crystal, rotating in a cavern at the very heart of the mountain.

"You have news for us?" inquired Jofre. He rose from his chair as Mandor and Nanchez bowed. This council of five ruled the city in the mountain but everyone knew that one leader stood above the others in ambition, vision, ferocity, and absolute power.

Mandor stammered as he stared into Jofre's white eyes, "Yes, Master. We believe that we're about fifteen feet from breaking through."

"Have you stopped the digging?" asked The Master.

"Yes," said Nanchez.

"Good. The *seer* has determined that our mission must be undertaken when there is no moon. The first dark night is tomorrow. You will have the tunnel ready as soon as the light fades."

"Yes, Master," said Mandor and Nanchez together.

"You are dismissed," commanded Jofre, as he sat down silently, waiting as the two men bowed, turned, and marched to the entry. The small woman pushed the doors closed behind them, withdrawing her key from the slot, and resumed her station outside.

The following evening, Mandor and Nanchez stood close to the face of the machine, as it pulverized the last layers of dense black stone. Suddenly, the rock fell forward, away from the grinding plate, and they could see a patch of indigo sky and stars glowing in the twilight. The workers backed the machine down the track and cleared away enough rock to crawl through the opening.

The mouth of the tunnel opened on a narrow outcrop, about halfway up the side of the mountain. From here, they could see the entire eastern plains dotted with tiny farmhouses, the light from their windows glowing securely, faint embers soon to fade in a new darkness. The ridge tore away to the south, a writhing serpent silhouetted against the faintest flush of color fading in the west. "Soon, this will be ours," said Mandor, hugging Nanchez with one arm. "Let's clear the workers out of the tunnel." They turned back into the hole in the rock and began to shout, "Everybody out, Now!"

The workers fell into formation and marched down the tracks into fresh cool air at the north entrance. Mandor and Nanchez were clearing rubble from the entrance when they heard footsteps approaching. The five Masters appeared in the darkness, walking in a tight circle surrounding the *seer* so closely that the only part that could be seen was a pair of tiny boots marching in lockstep with the Masters. A shock of straight white hair flashed between the giant men, as they walked through pools of light boring down through the darkness.

"I ordered everyone cleared from the tunnel!" shouted the first Master. "Move to the side and leave after we have passed!"

Jofre brought up the rear of the column and turned to nod approvingly at Mandor and Nanchez. They bowed and trudged down the tunnel.

"You can not accompany me," said the *seer*, in a small whisper.

"I know but I wish I could. I'd feel better if you were not doing this alone," said Jofre, staring down at the *seer's* electric blue eyes charged with respect and duty but certainly nothing more.

The *seer* turned without responding and climbed through the opening while the five Masters stood in formation and waited silently.

An hour passed and then two. At one point, the *orbs* in the tunnel dimmed for a few moments but regained their chilling purple glow. The five men did not shift from their stance, although one might have sensed their impatience. Finally, there was the crunch of loose rock outside the hole and the *seer* reappeared. She was smiling.

"Is it done?" inquired Jofre.

"Yes," replied the *seer*. "I'm sure the Keeper will be seeing results directly."

"You'll be remembered as the savior of our people," said Jofre, with a slight bow, "for initiating this first step along the path to reclaim our destiny."

The tiny blond blushed but did not smile, "I serve at the pleasure of the Council."

The five men surrounded the *seer* and marched back down the tunnel, in the distance a clap of thunder echoed across the island.

Mandor and Nanchez stood just outside the entrance, as the five Masters passed. The Council marched in lockstep, a posture that implied the success of the *seer's* mission. The procession stopped in formation without breaking the seal around the tiny *seer*. The mystique and secret identity of the *seer* was maintained for all but a tiny elite circle of power within the population.

The first Master said, "Nanchez, your systems await you. The progression has been initiated. Mandor, place guards at the outer entrance to the tunnel, do not allow anyone to scale the other side of the mountain. Let the order be death on sight!" The Masters continued along the quay into their sanctified chambers behind the mechanical wing.

Chapter Nine

Adrian was jolted awake by a deafening clap of thunder that rattled the glass in the open windows of his bedroom. His feet were on the floor before his eyes registered the flash. He gathered the billowing drape and sealed the sash against rain rushing horizontally in waves crashing through the night. The wind was howling, huge trees bowing to the east then heaving back to the west under daggers of purple lightning tracing across the sky. "This is going to be some storm," he thought, as he latched the window, grabbed an *orb*, and charged down the stairs.

Before he reached the first landing, he could hear George yelling into the *messenger*, "What's going on?"

Professor Ponte's voice crackled and his image faded in and out on the screen. "I don't know," he screamed, "it's the Balance. The Crystal is out of balance!" His image faded into static and then reappeared, "I wish we had a *seer!*"

George turned, as Adrian stepped into the room, and stared intently at his nephew, who was dripping on the carpet, as if seeing the boy for the first time, "Professor, there is only one person on the island that we haven't tested…Adrian."

"Well, it's worth a try. He does have the lineage," crackled the voice from the *messenger*. "Bring him to me!"

Adrian felt the hairs on the back of his neck prickle and a cold chill ran up his wet nightshirt. He certainly had no understanding of what they were talking about but his senses were primed in anticipation.

"Adrian," said George, in an unusually intense voice, "please, sit down. We need to talk."

Adrian sat on the edge of the chair facing George's desk, shivering as an icy shawl of frigid air settled around him.

"Do you remember Simian from my story about Atlantis?" he asked, draping a blanket around the boy's shoulders.

"Yes," said Adrian.

"There were no *seers* in our generation and we've tested every child on the island. None of them are *seers*. Do you remember that the power of the *seer* can be passed through the mother?" he asked.

"Yes," said Adrian.

"Well, Elsie and your mother are the only women on this side of the island who are direct descendants of that line, which makes you a possible candidate. Would you be willing to take a test?"

Adrian was quiet for a moment. What was he being asked to do? He was still a boy. How could he take on the responsibility of being a *seer*, whatever that meant? "I'd be willing to do whatever I can," he said, quietly.

"At this point, the test won't ask too much of you. If you understand the characters in the Book of Wisdoms, then you are a *seer*. If not...well, then you're not," said George.

"OK," said Adrian, feeling slightly relieved. How could he possibly understand a book that no one else could read?

"Off you go then, get dressed and we'll head up to the Professor's"

George pulled the trolley around to the kitchen door and Adrian charged down the steps and jumped into the open door. His uncle closed the cover over the open cab but the howling wind was blowing so hard that they were both soaking wet before the trolley passed through the gate.

The truck rushed forward and then slowed. No matter how George steered the vehicle, it bounded off in different directions on its own. "The vector's out of whack!" With the driving rain, the wind, and the lack of any real control over the trolley, the journey took almost twice as long as their last trip to the observatory for the astronomy class.

Finally, the glow of the lights at the base of the rock column appeared. The Professor was standing in the doorway.

"Here, dry yourselves," said Ester, handing the towels to George and Adrian, as they ran up the steps.

"Come along, then," cried Professor Ponte, as he waddled into the parlor. "There isn't a moment to waste!"

A sputtering fire crackled reluctantly in the fireplace and Tic the cat settled on the back of one of the sofas, gazing at Adrian intently, "So, you think you can help?"

"I don't know," replied Adrian, "but I'm willing to try."

The cat arched his back and rubbed up against Adrian's chest, "Understanding is demanding." He looked up into the boy's eyes, "I hope that you are the one."

The Professor led them to the broad oak table in the dining room. A large book sat in the center, unlike any volume that Adrian had ever seen. The gold cover reflected the light from the *orb* hanging from the ceiling, a cross and crescent deeply etched in the smooth surface. He felt a tingling current when he touched the golden clasp and ran his fingers around the seam along the front and back covers but there was no evidence of pages between.

The Professor's hand glowed in reflection as he caressed the golden tome, "This is the Book of Wisdoms," he said quietly. "Please open the volume and tell me what you see."

Adrian reached for the edge of the heavy cover and laid it back on the table. Inside, he found two pages faced with a thin sheet of golden crystal or glass. Strange symbols, more like Egyptian hieroglyphs than letters or words, marched in formation to the edge of each page and then set off in random directions. There was a pattern in their movements but it was beyond Adrian's comprehension.

The Professor, Ester, and George stood in silence, while Adrian stared intensely at the figures wandering before him who seemed to be daring him to find the magic word to get beyond the introduction or opening page preceding any real information. Finally, he asked, "You said that this was something like a computer...that you have to ask a question?"

"Yes, that's true," said the Professor, his index finger pressed to his lips. "Ask it whether The Crystal is out of balance."

Adrian stared down at the characters moving around the pages. "What is wrong with The Crystal?" he asked.

The movement on the page stopped. Adrian looked up at the Professor, who had a very small smile at the corners of his lips. "You've asked the wrong question," he said. "Ask it whether The Crystal is out of balance."

"Is The Crystal out of balance?" asked Adrian to the book. The figures rushed about the page again to line up in formations that formed the word 'Yes'. He looked up at the Professor, his eyes filled with excitement, confusion, and a bit of terror. "It says, 'Yes'."

The Professor and George had pumped him with questions for hours and Adrian's mind was tired. Sometimes the figures would form a word, at others, they would point in a direction or a symbol would materialize. As often as not, they would continue to march around the page, ignoring the boy, until the precise question was asked. Translating the responses was becoming easier, as Adrian worked, but he was beginning to feel the strain.

Ester brought fruit, cookies, and juices, "It's time you gave this young man a break. You've been at this for hours."

"Right you are," said the Professor, with only the slightest hint of impatience.

Adrian got up from the table and wandered around the parlor. The fury of the storm howled outside the windows, fierce and angry. He stood in front of the smoldering fire in a vain attempt to warm his hands and gazed around at the library of books, the dancing skeleton, the bits and pieces of the Professor's inventions in various stages of completion or abandonment, and the stars of the early morning sky.

Tic rose from his nap, stretched, and walked over the furniture until he was standing in front of Adrian. "So you are a *seer*," he said, with a cock of his head. "I knew that you were special the first time you came into this room."

"Well, thank you," said Adrian. "My mother thinks that I'm pretty special too."

"Well, she should. You realize the responsibility that goes with this talent of yours?"

"What do you mean?"

"You are the only *seer* on this side of the island. That is a responsibility to everyone who lives here."

Adrian stared into the cat's amber eyes. How could he be talking to a cat, let alone be a *seer*, and he still had no idea of what being a *seer* really meant beyond translating from the Book. Nothing in his life hinted that he was different or special. He was just a boy who wanted to grow up to be a man in the image of his father.

Tic sat down, the tip of his tail twitching, "Yes, there is a responsibility for this new talent of yours…at a price more dear than you might imagine."

George and the Professor sat in quiet conversation at the table with the closed book, while Adrian wandered around the room, dazed and confused by the tomcat's revelation. "Are you ready for another try?" asked George.

"Yes, sir," said Adrian, taking his seat at the table before the book.

"We think that we haven't been asking the right questions," said the Professor. "Would you ask it whether the Others have anything to do with the imbalance?"

"Are the Others responsible for the imbalance?" Adrian asked the book. The figures stopped moving for a moment and then rushed around the page to form the word "Yes."

The Professor looked concerned. "Ask it if they have tampered with the third crystal."

"The third crystal?" asked George.

"Well, yes," said the Professor. "There is a third crystal, somewhere on the mountain. It maintains the equilibrium between the Golden Crystal and the Black Crystal. If it has been moved or damaged, I don't know what the consequences might be."

"The results might include a huge storm over the island, unlike any that we've seen before? Waves in the cove that have sunk two of the trawlers and washed over the shops in the village...or geysers gushing straight up out of the ground, where no water has ever been produced before...or snow covering our end of the island...or vectors that no longer move in straight lines?" asked George.

"Well, yes. Any or all of those," said the Professor quietly.

"What can be done about it?" asked George.

"We'll have to ask the book."

Adrian asked the question and the figures moved like swarming bees around the page. Finally, they stopped. The answer was "Yes".

"Ok," said the Professor. "Ask it if the third crystal has been damaged or replaced."

Adrian repeated the Professor's question. The figures stopped moving for a moment and then formed a diamond on the page...the gem turned black.

The Professor sat back in his chair, removed his too small glasses, and rubbed his tired eyes. He pursed a knuckle to his lips, staring at George and Adrian, "We've learned all that we will learn from The Book. They've taken control of the balance," he said quietly. "I think it's time for us to introduce our young *seer* to the Crystal."

The Professor toddled to the elevator, the doors opened, and they stepped inside. This time the elevator fell like a rock into a well. Finally, it bumped to a stop and the carved doors opened into a large blazingly white room.

Adrian's first impression was that he had stepped inside a giant glaring neon egg. The white floor curved into walls, which arched into the ceiling around a huge Crystal, whirling at a fantastic rate, its axis wobbling above a single point on the floor. It reminded Adrian of a child's spinning top, except this monster looked as if shards of golden glass had been patched together by some gargantuan force.

An intense amber light burned within the core of the gem. Adrian shielded his eyes, awed and frightened by the power emanating from the center of the room that enveloped the boy in a warm embrace, enticing him across the smooth white cavern to the huge stone.

A thick dust formed on the smooth surface beneath the jewel. It shimmered like golden frost on an early winter morning, reflecting the light cascading down from The Crystal.

"Gold dust," said George. "This is how we pay for the things we need from the mainland."

Adrian looked at his uncle in disbelief, thinking, "A Crystal that creates gold dust… endlessly? The trawler that turned south!" He asked, "Will it ever stop producing the gold?"

"It will if we don't find a solution to this problem," said George, "but then it won't matter, if we don't find a way to correct the imbalance, the southern part of the island will die."

"I'm afraid the whole island will be destroyed, just like Atlantis, if the Keeper on the other end of this loses control," said Ponte.

The Professor put his small fat hand on Adrian's shoulder and looked at him through his too-small glasses, the knuckle of a chubby finger at his lips, "There is something that I must ask of you and you may decline if you choose. No one, including me, would think the less of you."

Adrian looked back into his wise but desperate eyes. He knew that he was not going to like what was coming next because there would not be an 'or' in the request.

"The *seer* can enter the crystal. Although, I'm not sure that any *seer* has ever entered it when it was in this condition. It could be dangerous but there is no other way to find the solution to this problem. The books have given us as much information as we'll get. You are the *seer*, the only one who can accomplish this task. No one else on the island has the power or the perception."

Adrian pointed up at The Crystal. "You want me to go inside of that?"

"Yes," said the Professor, gravely.

Adrian was quiet for a moment, "How?"

"Did you bring your key?"

The young *seer* reached into his pocket and withdrew the golden key, the gift from his mother. His parents flashed through his mind and he remembered her saying, "It will open doors for you."

"I've only seen this done once before, when old Justin entered it years ago, shortly after Paul disappeared." He crawled beneath the spinning crystal and brushed away a dune of gold dust, revealing a small slot.

"You must insert your key here," said the Professor, looking inquiringly at Adrian.

The boy wilted under Ponte's intense sincerity and turned to his uncle. George knelt down to his nephew with kindness in his eyes, "You can say no."

"No, I can't," said Adrian. "From what you two have told me, there is no other choice but for me to enter this gigantic crystal to find the answer to this problem. No one else can do this?"

"No," said George.

Adrian looked up at the giant Golden Crystal. Slowly, he knelt down and inserted his key. A booming voice asked, "Who are you?"

"I am Adrian, Sara's son. I am told that I am a *seer*."

"If you are not a *seer* you will die as you enter within," said the very loud voice.

"I have no other choice," replied Adrian.

The Crystal did not respond but seemed to speed its rotation faster and faster, until the facets blurred and a dark oval formed on the whirling surface, slowly expanding until it reached six feet tall and, perhaps, two feet wide at its center.

"You will enter The Crystal now!" said the voice. Adrian turned to look at the two men, who stared back at him, their mouths open, their eyes wide. He took a deep breath and stepped onto the flat surface beneath the crystal, shuddered, and put one foot inside the breach. He took the next step and the white room disappeared.

Adrian looked at his feet, struggling to balance on a small smooth crystal that glowed with blinding intensity. He peered around the inside of a huge crystalline bubble, larger than it appeared from the outside, and spinning even faster, as if he was standing in the eye of a golden tornado.

Larger cousins of the figures from the Book of Wisdoms floated above the inside surface of the crystal whizzing past in the background without affecting their movements. They appeared more three-dimensional than those on the glass pages and each figure shifted independently of the others, marching up and down and around the entire circumference in some random regimented pattern. He stood very still and waited.

The large voice enveloped him, although he could not be sure whether his ears were hearing the sound or his mind was capturing the message from the powers inside the giant Crystal. "So you are a *seer*!"

"I believe that is true. I think I'm still alive!" Adrian replied.

"We will see about that!" said the voice and then there was silence, except for the rush of air dashing around the chamber.

The figures stopped marching and filed to the sides, although the Crystal continued to spin erratically behind them. A clear patch opened in front of Adrian and a globe appeared. He guessed that it might be Earth before the original landmass, Pangaea, slowly pealed apart over millennia into drifting continents. The globe rotated slowly on a tilted axis and small red and black dots glowed here and there across the surface.

The voice interrupted the white noise inside the sphere, "When the Earth was born, powerful Crystals formed at pressure points between the tectonic plates. Over the eons, some were destroyed by the movement of those landmasses, others were buried under mountains or deep beneath the seas. A few lifted to the surface. They were always formed in threes. One positive, another negative, and a smaller stone to provide stability."

The globe continued to turn, slowly, and the single land mass unfolded to form the continents. Some of the dots disappeared.

"As man developed and progressed, he found some of these points and a few societies used the powers of The Crystals to promote the balance of life. Others found the negative Crystals and used those energies to disrupt the equilibrium of nature. Where these powers were misused or abused, The Crystals were destroyed."

As the globe continued to rotate, some of the red lights glowed fiercely and faded. Their twins blazed a violent purple-black and were extinguished, leaving fewer places where the dots continued to pulse. "Very few men have reached a true understanding of the powers of The Crystals and most were blind to the potential. Where they maintained the balance between the requirements of man and the needs of nature, life flourished. In those places where man became too greedy for the power provided by The Crystals, the gems disintegrated and their civilizations disappeared."

"When all of The Crystals have been destroyed, life as you know it will cease to exist." the voice continued.

The globe disappeared and, again, there was silence.

A black Crystal appeared before Adrian, spinning in reverse of the Golden Crystal that encased him, but it glowed with a deep purple luminance. Adrian felt an intense negative energy flowing into the black gemstone. He wanted to step back but there was no room behind him, so he stood very still, his knees quaking and blood rushing from his head.

"The Others, as you call them, have disrupted The Balance on this island. You, and only you, must repair the damage."

"But..." stammered Adrian.

"They have replaced the third gem with a black Crystal. You must find that stone and replace it with the rainbow Crystal."

"Where do I find the third Crystal?" asked Adrian.

"It is high on the mountain, at the center of the knot. You will know it when you see it."

"And the 'rainbow' Crystal?"

"Ask the Keeper of the Powers. We sense that he used one in his machines nearby. Remember, you and only you can replace the balancing Crystal. If anyone accompanies you, you will fail. You must hurry before the imbalance becomes irreversible."

The voice disappeared and the figures again marched around the inside of the spinning gemstone. The dark opening appeared next to him and he tumbled onto the smooth white surface outside The Crystal. He looked up and saw George and the Professor frozen exactly where they had been when he entered the enormous stone. They were staring at him and their mouths were still hanging open.

His muscles went limp, the cavern started spinning, and the boy collapsed in the gold dust glimmering on the floor beneath the spinning Crystal.

———✺✺✺———

Adrian regained consciousness lying on the sofa in the parlor with Ester sopping his forehead with a cold, damp towel. He looked up to find the Professor, George, and Tic the cat staring down at him.

"Are you alright?" asked Ester, quietly.

"I think so. What happened?"

"You emerged from The Crystal and collapsed with a mighty thump. We thought you were dead," said the Professor.

"What happened inside?" asked George.

Adrian struggled to sit up, hesitating midway while his eyes focused and the spinning subsided. He rubbed a large knot on his forehead and stared at his fingers, sparkling with gold dust.

"Here dear, keep this cool cloth on that bump. I'll get some ice," said Ester as she handed him the mop.

Adrian sat back into the sofa and took a deep breath to settle himself. "Did you hear the voice?" he asked.

"The voice?" asked George.

"Yes, the voice from inside The Crystal."

"No, we didn't hear a voice. You started yelling at the Crystal and disappeared inside. It seemed only moments before you re-emerged, a bit wobbly I must say, then fell and banged your head."

"The voice said that the Others had replaced the third crystal with a black crystal."

The Professor and George glanced at each other and then back to Adrian.

"It said that I have to replace the black crystal with a rainbow crystal. It also said that you used a rainbow crystal in one of your machines," said Adrian, trying desperately to focus on the Professor, who seemed to be swaying closer then farther away.

Ponte smiled, "Yes, I know the crystal. I used it to control the power in the village. It seemed appropriate. We'll have some work to do to extract it."

"It also said that I must replace the crystal alone, that no one could go with me, and, if they did, I would not find it," said the boy, anxiously.

"Did it say where the third crystal is located?" asked George.

"Yes, it is on the mountain, at the center of the knot."

"We can get you there!" cried the Professor.

Adrian sank into the sofa. His head was throbbing and the blurry vision made his stomach queasy.

"Come along, George, I'll need your help," said the Professor. "Ester, look after our young *seer*. We'll be back shortly."

The two men returned to the elevator and disappeared. Ester

made Adrian lie down and brought some juice and a steaming bowl of broth. The young *seer* sipped the cool drink and decided that eating might not be the best choice at the moment. He closed his eyes and drifted into a troubled sleep filled with shadowy figures slogging through a vicious storm in the darkness.

George and Ponte descended into the depths beneath the rock pillar, stepped into the chamber, where the Golden Crystal was still spinning madly, and turned to the right through a short hallway past several storage rooms to an old worn office door with rippled glass and into the Professor's workshop.

Along one wall of a long narrow room, a row of mysterious machines sputtered and wheezed, while down the other, *orbs* of various sizes were suspended in midair with wires running from one gadget to the next and an endless variety of unusual tools dropped haphazardly on a battered workbench. The Professor led George to the back of the room and stopped before a large, gray metal cabinet. He opened the doors to reveal a mass of wires of every color connecting one module to another, a jumble of multicolored spaghetti packed the inside of the cabinet. In the center was a heavy metal casing, buried under the muddle of cables and other components. A red light blinked rapidly on the outside of the casing.

"It'll be a job to extract the crystal. It's inside this shielded casing," said the Professor.

"What's the red light?" asked George.

"It means the system is out of kilter...but we might have assumed that, considering what's happening outside," replied the Professor.

"Let's get to it then," said George.

It took several hours to shut down the system and burrow through the wires, which blossomed from bundles spewing from the casing. George and Ponte were sweating profusely, as they finally pulled the heavy shell from the cabinet with a loud clang as they dropped it the last few inches to the floor. George looked concerned, "Sorry, I lost my grip."

"I think it'll be alright. I made the casing to hold the immense energy of this crystal, so it should have protected it," said the Professor.

He toddled to the other end of his workbench to collect some tools and, after another hour, removed the top of the shell to reveal a large crystal and gently pulled the gem from its mount. It glinted brightly in the dim light of the workshop and George noticed that its facets reflected every color of the rainbow. The Professor wrapped the heavy crystal in a large cloth and carried it back to the elevator, leaving the guts of the machine scattered about the floor.

The crimson cross and crescent, emblazoned across a white spinnaker, blossomed in a strong southwesterly breeze, driving the Sparrow north into the Pacific from the Panama Canal. John and Sara were fit and deeply tanned after sailing through the tropics and the strange encounter with the old man at the market stall in Montego Bay merely amplified a sense of adventure as they tacked into the final leg of the passage, with a few days in San Francisco before continuing on to Vancouver.

John sat cross-legged on the deck, tracing a course across the charts, while Sara manned the helm of the beautiful sloop, "We can hug the coast most of the way."

His wife smiled down at him, blue eyes twinkling like sunlight on clear waters, fingering the tiny locket dangling from a slender golden chain around her neck with one hand, while heaving the tiller to catch just a little more air with the other, "We've been lucky, so far. The weather has been with us the whole journey."

"The pilot at the canal mentioned a tropical storm brewing in the Gulf and pushing west. They're calling it Agatha and we'll have to keep an eye out for her."

"I'm reminded of the author and ominous tales of murder and

94

mayhem," laughed Sara.

Over the next few days, the clouds grew thick and dark, as they sailed up the Mexican coast. Mild and steady winds shifted around to the northeast as the intense low-pressure system pushed across Mexico, dragging heat and moisture from the Gulf. They hauled down the sheets, hoisted a slender storm jib, and cleated a smaller mainsail. John guided the elegant sloop away from the coast and, in spite of heavy seas, they were still making good time ahead of the approaching hurricane. He was gambling they could outrun it.

On the forth night, Sara woke her husband from a very sound sleep, "The winds are howling and the waves are frightening," she yelled above the din, trembling in panic.

The Sparrow heaved to port and John slid off the bunk, "Let's drop the mainsail." He pulled on his yellow slicker and scrambled up the ladder to the deck.

Black translucent mountains towered over the floundering sloop and The Sparrow seemed very fragile, as it was driven from deep valleys onto the immense crown of the next swell. A fierce wind ripped huge sheets of water off the crests of the waves and rain rushed with ocean spray to form a dense cloud swirling around the tiny vessel, each droplet a stinging dart charged by a whirlwind. Their running lights seemed faint sparks in a churning darkness interrupted by flashes of lightning tracing across the sky, icy fingers scrambling to touch the edge of a savage night.

They pulled down the mainsail and tied it off but The Sparrow continued to list to port, as John steered her into the oncoming surge of black water to avoid being swamped by a following wave overtaking the stern.

With a loud crack, a fierce gust shredded the jib and loosed a tangle of lines thrashing around the mast, bullwhips flicking and slashing with vicious intent. Like a child's toy, the violent power of the giant swells lifted the yacht to the roiling summit and pitched her racing down a massive breaker into an oncoming liquid mountain, as a following wave collapsed over the stern and knocked Adrian's parents into the well. John scrambled to reach the tiller and heaved it hard to starboard but too late, a second surge, much larger than the last, collapsed on the beautiful sailboat. A bolt of lightning exploded across the sky as the bow rose into the fierce gale. The mast shattered into a thousand deadly shards, driven by a third wave crashing over the sloop from port, and The Sparrow disintegrated into tiny fragments swallowed by a dark and angry sea.

———◦❀◦❀◦———

Adrian awoke to find George and the Professor seated in two aging stuffed chairs poking at a reluctant fire and talking quietly. The storm raged against the windows of the old stone house and lightning shattered the darkness under the incessant growl of thunder.

"The *messengers* are unreliable and I need to talk with Elsie before we allow Adrian to attempt this venture, even if he is a reluctant volunteer. Besides, we'll need to go back to our house for clothing and supplies before we head up to the mountain." Turning to Adrian, George inquired. "Are you up to it?"

"I think so," said Adrian, straining to sit up. His head was still spinning and the bump on his forehead throbbed like a mallet striking a bass drum from the inside out.

"I'm not sure whether the trolley will work, with the vector system as it is. It should move but it probably won't follow the paths," said the Professor.

"We'll make it," said George. "We'll be back as soon as we can."

George reached out to help Adrian stand. They pulled on their coats and hesitated as the front door opened to a gale, matured into an angry and deadly tempest driving wet snow horizontally.

Tic ran between their legs and out the door. "Tic, come back," shouted Ester into the torrent but the cat disappeared.

The ride back to the House of the Four Seasons was even more frantic than their trip that morning. The trolley moved along normally for a few hundred yards, then careened from side to side and, at some points, spun in circles before righting itself and moving off again. Adrian glanced at George, who was hanging on to the steering wheel with both hands. His knuckles were white and creases etched his forehead, furrowed by the strain of concentration. Adrian decided that his uncle was not in the proper humor to carry on a conversation and the chaotic movements of the truck enhanced the woozy gyrations inside his head.

The trolley pulled up to the kitchen steps and they scrambled through the rain into the house. Elsie and the girls met them at the door with towels to dry them off. "Are you alright dear?" asked Elsie, looking up into her husband's eyes.

Turning to Adrian, she asked, "What is this knot on your forehead?"

"I fell," said Adrian simply, avoiding an explanation the events of the past several hours.

"Well, come along then, we'll tend to that. Let's get you into some dry clothes."

"We'll be heading back to the Professor's," said George.

"You'll be what?" asked Elsie, in disbelief. "This weather isn't fit for man nor beast and, at the moment, I'm not sure which category you two fit into!"

"I'll explain. Girls, would you take Adrian up and find him some warm dry clothes, and then find some gloves, boots, and a slicker. Elsie, would you fix us something to eat, while I go change my clothes?"

The girls guided a woozy Adrian out of the kitchen, into the foyer, each clutching an arm. His legs were rubbery, his body exhausted.

Elsie took George's hand and squeezed tightly, "We need to talk before you go anywhere!"

As the children slowly descended the stairs, they could hear George shouting into the *messenger* on the desk in his study, "What do you mean they've disappeared?"

The twins turned into the kitchen and sat with Adrian at the table, which was now covered with all sorts of temptations. He reached for a peach and ate hungrily.

"Feeling any better?" asked Elsie.

"A little," said Adrian. "I think some food will help."

The girls sat, chins in hands, on the opposite side of the table, staring at Adrian. Neither said a word.

George shuffled back into the kitchen. He was still wearing his wet clothing and looked more disheveled than when they arrived back at the farmhouse. He slumped into his chair at the end of the oval table and covered his face with his hands. "Adrian," he began quietly, his voice trailing off.

Adrian stared anxiously, trying to read his mind.

"Oh, Adrian," said George. "I don't know how to say this, especially with all that's happened today. My boy, The Sparrow is missing. Your parents left the Panama Canal and headed north. A hurricane blew out of the Gulf of Mexico and there has been no word from them since."

Adrian's mouth dropped open. "Are they...?" he began.

"We don't know what's happened, I'm trying to find out," said George quietly.

Tear's spilled down his cheeks, as he pushed away from the table and ran up the stairs to his room.

After a while, Elsie knocked gently on the door, "May I come in?"

Adrian did not reply. He was lying face down on his bed, sobbing into his pillows, hugging his teddy bear tightly. His aunt walked quietly across the room and sat on the edge of the bed, reached out to rub Adrian's back, feeling the sobs shuddering through his body. Finally, he sat up and Ester wrapped her arms around him and held him very close.

They rocked back and forth, Adrian's face buried in his aunt's shoulder. Gushing tears wet the fabric of her dress.

"I don't know what to say to you," said Elsie, quietly. "You've been through an awful lot today. We don't know what's happened to your parents and I honestly wish that I had a better way of putting that. They could be fine and just blown off course...or, well, we just don't know."

"George told me about what happened at the observatory. You are a brave young man to even consider entering The Crystal and no one would blame you, if you were to decline whatever the rest of this involves. We all love you."

Adrian didn't respond. He was so lost in his thoughts, his worries about his parents, that he had pushed all consideration of Crystals and ancient Books out of his mind. Horrible visions raged in his heart and, in this moment, he wanted to sit alone in the dark for a very long time.

After a while, he pulled away from his aunt and looked deeply into her blue eyes, exactly like his mother's eyes, although a little older, a little wiser. A sob welled up from deep inside, "I...I...I can't let you down..."

"Darling, you won't be letting us down. You've already done enough. From what you learned, George and the Professor know what's happened. Perhaps they can find another way to solve the problem."

"There.....is.....no.....other way. The Crystal told me that I, and I alone, am the only one on the island who can replace the black crystal."

He rested his head against her shoulder and was quiet for a while, his mind racing between terrifying thoughts of his parents, imagining all the tragic things that might have happened, and the past hours at the Professor's house. When he closed his eyes, the inside of The Crystal whizzed around him in a golden blur chased by an echo of the voice, "You must hurry before the imbalance becomes irreversible."

He pulled away from Elsie again and looking into her soft, warm face. "I have no other choice. I have to find and replace the black crystal and I need to do it now."

Chapter Ten

Molly and Megan provided a heavy sweater, gloves, heavy boots, and a slicker for Adrian, hugged him tightly, and looked terribly worried. "Please be careful!"

As Adrian and George rushed through the storm to the trolley, Brandy and Tic jumped into the back.

The young *seer* spun around, "How did you two get here?"

"We're coming with you," said Tic.

"You stowed away when we left the observatory!"

"It was easy. Neither of you even turned around to look back here. From what you were saying at the Professor's, no one can go with you to find the black crystal. We interpret that to mean that no human can accompany you. The Crystal didn't say anything about the other living creatures on this island. This is our home. We're going too."

Adrian and George turned at each other with the same thought. It made no sense to dump the animals out into the gale and they could use all the help they could find. The blizzard was churning violently as they slogged north from the House of Four Seasons through wet snow and ice. The trolley fought to follow the vectors, spinning and dancing from one side of the path to the other. Finally, the dim lights of the Professor's windows appeared in the distance. The door flew open as they slid to a stop and the Professor emerged, rubbing his hands together, looking frantic, "The Crystal is wobbling even more than when you left. I fear that we are running out of time!"

"Nice to see you too, Ponte," said George as they pushed through the door, followed by Brandy and Tic.

"Oh, there you are," said Ester, grabbing the cat and clutching him to her breast. "And you two, we've been worried about you."

"Thank you," said George.

Ester turned to Adrian, who was standing aside with his head bowed, "Are you alright, Adrian?"

"He's been through even more than you know. I'll explain later. In the meantime, do you have the rainbow crystal ready?"

"Yes, yes," said the Professor. "I've put it in this sling you can wear over your shoulder. That should leave your hands free. I've also found this small *orb* to light your way. Ester has made some food and I suggest we get going before things get any worse."

Adrian, the Professor, George, Tic, and Brandy ran through a deluge of ice pellets and jumped into the trolley. George turned the vehicle around and headed north along the icy track to the base of the black mountain.

Ester stood in the doorway watching the glow of the *orbs* on the back of the trolley fade into the blizzard, she turned and walked back into a cold and empty parlor. Her anxious eyes behind the too large glasses danced around the room and came to rest on the cages of the birds. She walked over to the pens, flipped the latches, and opened the doors. She turned and marched over to the glass enclosures that confined the snakes, which still gave her the shivers, and lifted the cover off each cage.

"You might as well go too!" she shouted. "Get out, Go! All of you! Help them!"

Mandor and Nanchez ran to the chambers of the Masters where the same small woman stood at attention before the massive doors.

"We have to speak with the Masters. Our guards have spotted movement on the south side of the mountain!" said Mandor.

"Excuse me," she said, turning away to talk softly into a tiny *messenger* on her wrist. After a moment, she turned back to them, inserted her key into the lock, and swung the doors open to allow them entry.

"You have news for us?" asked Jofre.

"Yes," stammered Mandor, "our guards have spotted lights moving at the southern base of the mountain."

"They can't do anything. They don't have a *seer*, so they'll never find the third crystal. Our *seer* assured us of that before we started this mission."

"Either way, we would like to increase the guard," said Nanchez.

"You have our permission. Place another two-dozen men across the bluff, as well as along the trails on the east and west coasts, with orders to use extreme measures with anyone attempting to reach the knot. Report anything unusual immediately."

The two men bowed, turned, and marched to the door.

"Before you go," said Jofre, "we'll be delivering the ultimatum in the morning. Will you be ready to capture all of the powers once they capitulate?"

Nanchez bowed, "Yes, Master."

The trolley pitched and rolled from side to side on slick furrowed ice covering the rough cart path from the moment they left the Professor's house. Other than the *orbs* on the trolley, darkness cloaked the northern plain, save streaks of savage lightning flashing across drifts of snow, mounding into dunes at the base of the mountain. Bruised from the rugged ride, it felt good to stand, even in a freezing gale. Jagged daggers of glistening black rock soared straight up and disappeared in the whirling white haze scouring the mountain.

"I wish we could go with you, Adrian," said George. "I feel irresponsible letting you do a man's job...alone."

"I know but we have no other choice," said Adrian, shivering. "Where do I go?"

The Professor pointed above the center of the mountain.

"You'll want to go up there, just above and to the right of that cliff. Wait for the lightning and I'll point to it." Lightning flashed close by with a mighty crack, illuminating the clouds of snow that shrouded most of the mountain. "There!" yelled the Professor, pointing up into the blizzard. "Do you see it?"

"Yes," replied Adrian, although he was not sure whether he had seen the knot or snow blowing through the air. From the angle that Professor Ponte pointed, he guessed the crystal was more than two-thirds of the way up the mountain and off to the right of center.

"There are two very large shiny rocks that have been pushed together to form a pointed arch above another pair forming the return. It's quite possible that the equalizing stone is hidden in that hollow at the center of the knot.

I've looked at this mountain through a telescope many times and I've noticed that the animals, who live on these peaks, always start their trek over here, behind this large boulder." He trudged through heavy snow to the right and closer to the vertical face of the rock, "I would guess that there might be an animal track behind it."

Just as he predicted, a slender gap opened into a steep, narrow path meandering up through the rocks.

"I guess this is where I leave you," said Adrian, looking up at the two men.

George knelt down and tucked the scarf tightly around Adrian's neck. He looked deep into the boy's eyes, "Are you sure about this?"

Adrian hesitated and George detected anxiety but not panic in the boy's eyes, "Yes."

He paused for a moment, with a twinge of guilt, "One more thing. If the Others have replaced the crystal, they might well have posted guards, so keep your eyes open." He hugged his nephew and stood, "We'll be here when you return."

Adrian waved and turned into the path, the rainbow crystal heavy in the sling across his back. Brandy sniffed the path and Tic ran ahead, disappearing into the blizzard.

He pulled the scarf up, leaving only a slit for his eyes, against giant snowflakes pelting his body in a pounding wind. The rocky path was glazed and slick, slowing their progress. Brandy stayed several yards ahead, sniffing the scents, leading the way up between twisting slippery slabs of black volcanic stone.

The Professor's small *orb* cast enough light to see the trail a few feet ahead. He followed Brandy's tracks and, here and there, found what must have been Tic's, crisscrossing the path. After they climbed a short way, he began to notice other tracks in the snow...animal tracks. Even partially covered with new snow, he recognized the prints of a deer or two, rabbits, what might be a fox, and perhaps some mountain goats. When he noticed larger tracks, he stopped, knelt down, and shined the light of the little *orb* across them. "These must have been made by a large cat...a very large cat," he thought. "I sure hope he's on our side!"

They struggled up through the rocks, stumbling and sliding. His hands were cold, wet, and bruised from falling when his boots slipped on the icy stones. Brandy continued to climb ahead and Adrian could only hope he would find the shortest path. Occasionally, he was startled by the cracking of branches in the trees, as limbs surrendered to the accumulating mass of ice and snow, falling, crashing to the ground with the roar of small explosions. The freezing wind numbed his face and tore at his jacket and, had he not been so determined, he was sure that it would not take long to die under these conditions.

After an hour, Brandy stopped and sat down in the middle of the narrow path between two large rocks, just above the tree line. Adrian caught up and crouched beside him. The setter's fur was coated with ice crystals and his feet were encased in snow. Adrian brushed the snow from his red fur and broke the snowballs that had accumulated between his toes. Brandy rubbed up against him but did not move.

"Are you OK?" asked Adrian.

"Yes," replied Brandy, "but we have to wait here. Tic will be back to meet us."

"How do you know?"

"See that small branch in the path?"

Just ahead, Adrian noticed a pine bough lying on top of the snow across the path. He crawled over to examine it and realized that it was freshly broken from a tree leaning over the trail.

"That means we are to wait here," said Brandy with a sniff. "He marked it."

Adrian opened his coat and snuggled close to the red dog, sharing what little warmth they had between them. After ten minutes, Tic leapt off a rock above them and landed next to Brandy.

"There are more than twenty guards spread out along the bluff, just above us. Do you see those faint purple lights moving back and forth?" asked Tic. Adrian leaned out from the protection of the huge slabs of stone that shielded them from view. Through the snow, dim magenta lights glowed through the snow cloud, as if many people were trying to scan the mountain below.

"I've asked some friends to help. The path that you want to follow leads off to the right. When you see a commotion up there, take off. Brandy will show you the way."

"Friends? What friends," asked Adrian?

"All of the animals on this island know each other. Sure, the snake eats the mouse and the hawk eats the snake, that is as nature intended, but we depend on each other. When our survival is threatened, we work together. This is that time," said Tic, shaking the snow off his coat. "Wait here."

The old tomcat bounded off up the path and disappeared into the storm. Adrian again leaned out to see what was happening on the cliff but Brandy grabbed his sleeve and pulled him back under the rocks, "Stay out of sight or they'll see us."

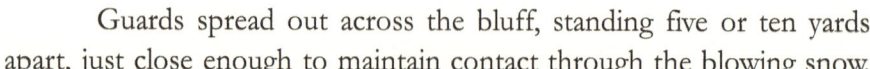

Guards spread out across the bluff, standing five or ten yards apart, just close enough to maintain contact through the blowing snow.

They were cold, wet, and miserable but absolutely dedicated to their duty, for fear is a discipline that commands obedience and loyalty. Powerful purple *orbs* shimmered brightly on clumps of snow and ice whirling around the mountain but the troops could not see more than a few yards down the side of the peak.

"No one in their right mind would try to climb this rock under these conditions," yelled the guard in the middle to his comrade on the left.

"So why are we out here, freezing?" replied the second guard.

"Because we were ordered to guard this entrance," laughed the first guard. "Besides, you know the consequences if we fail to follow our orders. That would be worse than this!"

"Right you are!"

The guard at the far end of the shallow ledge was shivering, convinced that this task would provide the first martyrs for the Council's righteous quest at the hands of the enemy or the weather. Buffeted by frigid wind and swirling snow charging the darkness, he could barely see his comrade and stood with his back against a crag in the rock where the shelf disappeared into a steep cliff that tumbled away into the whiteout. In spite of his black leather uniform and a heavy cloak gathered around his body, his teeth chattered and he cursed his duty and the Masters, "This is fit for neither of us!"

Behind and above him, he heard a very small, "Meow..." and turned to find a large black and white cat perched on top of a boulder. "What are you doing out here?" he asked, reaching up to grab the cat.

Just as the fingertips of the glove touched the fur on his flank, Tic disappeared and the largest mountain lion that the guard had ever seen materialized in his place. The huge cat extended his claws and leapt. Before the sentry tumbled backwards off the end of the bluff, the lion turned to the next guard and was on him in three steps, standing on his hind legs to smack the man in the face with each paw. The guard crumbled to his knees and rolled over the side.

The third guard in the line turned just in time to see his

comrade fall and the ferocious feline crouched, snarling, and ready to spring. The sentry grabbed a seeker stick from the sheath on his belt, slashing back and forth in front of the mountain lion until a snake shot out from the rocks in front of his eyes. He screamed and flailed the seeker stick around like a glowing baton, as poison fangs nipped into his cheek. The serpent darted back into the crevice and another curled around his ankle, pulling him screaming to the ground. The guard dropped his weapon, reaching his hands to the blood oozing from two small holes beneath his eye.

The guard, at the other end of the line, turned to find a beautiful buck standing within an arm's length. His jaw dropped. He had never been this close to a deer in his life and lacked the instinct to know whether to be afraid or in awe or both. In that moment of wonder, the beautiful creature lowered his antlers and took two quick steps. The guard never had a chance to block the blow with his lance before the deer flipped him down the side of the mountain.

The next two guards never saw the two hawks diving through the blizzard until their talons were extended just in front of the men's faces. They both fell to their knees. The two birds flew up into the air and swept back down to take out the next pair.

The animals attacked one or two at a time, until the final guards backed into the mouth of the tunnel as carnage cascaded across the bluff. The first guard, who was now partially protected, yelled, "I'll go for help!" He turned and ran down the tunnel.

"What about me?" yelled the other guard, left blocking the entrance. "You'd think they'd have installed *messengers* up here by now!"

"Stay put and don't let anyone or anything get past you!"

The guard backed into the passage, his seeker stick at the ready and primed to escape down the burrow at the first hint of attack.

Adrian and Brandy heard screams from the bluff and a purple

orb fluttered through the storm, landing on the path in front of them. "That's our cue," said Brandy. "Let's go!"

They leapt out from under the rocks and scrambled up the path that led off to the right. The wind whipped the face of the mountain and the snow was blinding. Brandy and Adrian dared not stop to survey the battle, as they passed the level of the bluff, and scampered up the slippery slope until the path ended on a shallow cliff.

"The other animals don't go near the knot. We'll just have to climb from here," said Brandy, who was panting hard.

Adrian was feeling the same fatigue. His whole body hurt from the effort and he knew that they still faced the most difficult leg of the climb. The scarf covering his nose and mouth was thick with ice crystals and his lungs clogged with frozen air, "Let's rest for a minute. I need to catch my breath!"

"Just for a moment. There will be more guards coming." They huddled together under an outcropping of rock. "At least we'll be ahead of them, if we hurry."

After a few minutes, Adrian squeezed Brandy, "I'm better, how about you?"

"Let's go."

The setter found the scent of the other *seer* and a slender breach through the rocks, straight up sheer slabs of stone glistening with ice. The red dog clawed at the slippery stone but slid back into the snowy crevice. Adrian picked him up and pushed him onto the next level and clamored up the ice but his boot caught in a crack and he pitched over backward, slamming his head on a protruding boulder.

The young *seer* awoke to a crashing tide searing through his skull behind his left ear and a bruise across his back from landing on the crystal. Brandy was standing over him, pulling at his scarf to lick his nose, "Are you alright?"

Adrian reached up and brushed the snow from the red dog's ear, "I'm feeling kind of woozy," he coughed, "but we still need to find the crystal."

"Can you sit up?"

He placed both hands on his head and sat up very slowly, the deep pounding of his pulse loud in his ears. His whole body shuddered from the cold and he leaned to retch on the snow.

"That's the second blow you've taken today. Are you sure you can go on?"

Adrian rubbed his teeth with a handful of snow, "We have no other choice. No one else can do this."

"Then we'd better get moving before we freeze and there are probably more guards around."

The boy rose very slowly, leaning against a slab of icy rock, trying to focus his eyes. The fierce rush of blowing snow was replaced by the skittering of ice pellets that would make the glassy coating on the rocks even more treacherous.

"Let's see if there's another path over here behind this boulder," said Brandy, shaking the snow off his coat and trotting along an impossibly narrow ledge above a precipitous drop into darkness. Adrian pressed his body against the cold rough stones and inched his feet across the slick sill, the storm and the mountain spinning around the throbbing pain inside his head. He lurched the last few steps before Brandy dragged him by the cuff of his sleeve to a cascade of fractured rocks spilling down from the next level. Adrian crumpled against a large boulder and retched again.

After a long, hard, rapid scramble, they found a depression under the two rocks that leaned together to form the base of the knot.

"I don't think that I can climb this one. You're on your own," panted Brandy.

Adrian brushed the snow from his back and dug ice pellets from between his toes, "You've been a great guide. Stay here and I'll be back." Brandy trotted over to the shelter of a hollow between the rocks and curled up against the cold.

The young *seer* looked up at the two massive shiny stones mashed together at a very steep angle and the ice covering the smooth surface looked slick. "Someone else scaled these rocks, there's got to be an easier way," thought Adrian, stuffing a glove between chattering teeth as he inched around the edge of the rock on the right only to find another sheer vertical face dropping into the storm. "Nothing here."

He turned and trudged back to his left, passing Brandy, his ears cocked and eyes following each step. Adrian eased around the end of the giant boulder and noticed loose rocks wedged behind the stone that fell away from the slope of the mountain to become the bottom of the knot. "A stairway!" He adjusted the sling on his back and began to climb.

Adrian struggled up the slippery slope, timing his movements between rushes of pain searing through his skull, before crawling onto a precipice, where the two giant rocks leaned together. In spite of heavy gloves, his hands were raw and there was no part of his body that was not cold, wet, and bruised. Exhausted, he hunched down for a moment, shivering violently. A vicious wind swirled around the peak, pelting him with snow and ice, and he felt that he could reach out to catch the handfuls of roiling clouds as they tumbled past. He wanted to close his eyes, to concentrate on the pain, but he knew that movement was life in this cold.

Two giant boulders, intertwined by some ancient upheaval into the top of the gargantuan knot, pulsed with the rhythm of the wrenching spasms behind his eyes. Adrian crawled to the back of the ledge, between the cleavage of the two upper stones, where he found a smooth surface and brushed the snow away.

The tip of a very large black diamond glowed eerie purple in the darkness. Four red crystals formed a quadrangle around it. The crown of the black diamond protruded from the surface but try as he might, he could not grasp it. He pulled off his gloves with chattering teeth, his hands slick and numb, but the radiant stone offered no edges.

"That's not going to work!" He sat back on his haunches and stared at the diamond. "There's got to be another way. Whoever was up here figured it out...I need something to pry it out." He reached under his coat and pulled his little penknife from his pocket but he could not break it loose, the fit was too fine to allow even a hair to slip between the stone and the clasp. He reached out, his fingers trembling uncontrollably, to try once more, and the four red crystals began to pulse. He pounded a crust of ice with the butt of his knife and found a small slot, right in front of him. He fumbled for his key and inserted it in the hole. The four crystals stopped pulsing and began to glow.

A voice suddenly erupted from the rock in front of him, "Who are you?"

"I am Adrian, Sara's son, and I am a *seer*."

"Our balance has been disrupted."

"I know. I've come to mend it."

There was silence. "How do I remove the black diamond?" The voice offered no response.

Adrian looked down at the black diamond and the four crystals. He pushed on each of the red crystals in turn. Nothing happened. He tried to push them all at once. Still nothing. As he stared into the glow, he realized that the four red stones were placed at what he thought were north, south, east, and west. The four seasons!

He pressed on the farthest stone. The gem stopped glowing. He pressed on the closest stone and it dimmed. North, South...he pressed the one on his right and then the one to the left and the black diamond began to rise out of the rock.

As soon as the gleaming jewel protruded enough to get a grip, he pulled hard and it slipped free. It was very heavy. He carefully placed it on the snow at his knees and pulled the sling from his back. He extracted the rainbow crystal and gently placed it in the mount that contained the black diamond but it would not drop into the cavity. He pushed on it and nothing happened. He sat back and stared at the rainbow crystal.

He pushed the red stones in the same order that released the black diamond but the clasp did not budge. His teeth were chattering and his hands were blue. "I've come all this way," he thought, his brain aching and desperate. "There has to be something I'm missing."

Suddenly, a thought flew through his mind...try the reverse order...so he pushed west, east, south, and then north. The four red crystals began to pulse and the rainbow crystal slowly descended into the rock. He laughed out loud as his body crumpled in the snow. He stuffed the golden key into his pocket and reached out to touch the black diamond's beautiful mirrored facets. The pulsing in his head made the glittering mirrors fall in and out of focus and he felt consciousness slipping away...to rest, just for a moment...

The grating of a rock sliding on the slope roused him and he rolled over to find a small figure wearing a black leather uniform beneath a cloak crouched next to him. A knife blade flashed. Instinctively, he raised the black diamond to deflect the blow. The blade slid across the surface of the crystal and sliced the back of his left hand.

He jumped to his feet and held the black diamond like a club while applying pressure with his elbow to the gushing wound. The tiny assassin advanced and he struggled to crouch. "I have no weapon, nothing to defend myself with," he thought, eyeing the child's pocketknife lying in the snow. The young *seer* held the black diamond out away from his body, over the edge of the precipice. "Back up or I'll drop it!" he shouted. The figure hesitated, pondering the options...calculating the odds.

"Who are you?" yelled Adrian.

"I am Alius!" screamed the little fighter. She threw back the black cowl to reveal the most beautiful face that Adrian had ever seen. Her hair was as white as chalk and her skin was as pale as the snow whirling around them. She had high cheekbones, a tiny nose, and those same electric blue eyes, cold with sheer determination.

He held the black crystal farther over the edge of the rocks, his hand shaking with the cold and the pain, and he knew that he could not hold the black stone much longer, "Put your knife down on the ground, where I can see it," he said, struggling to sound steady.

Slowly, she knelt down and placed the knife on the snow at her feet. She looked up, "Now the stone."

He pulled the gem close to his body but made no attempt to put it down, "Why would you do this?"

"My people have lived in the shadows, in the cold, for generations. It is our turn to stand in the sunlight."

"Your people chose to leave the south side of the island."

"That happened long before I was born," she hissed. "It is our destiny to take back what we lost!"

"It might be your destiny but it is not your right. The people who live on the south side of the island have spent generations creating a paradise for everything and everyone who lives there," said Adrian. Blood dripping onto the cuff of his sleeve was steaming, freezing before droplets hit the snow, and his knees were shaking.

"And it will be ours!" she shouted, grabbing the knife and lunging. Impulsively, he raised his leg to break her momentum and swung the black diamond at her head. The knife raked his thigh in the same instant that the crystal collided with the side of her skull. They both collapsed to the ground.

Adrian struggled to the fallen girl, pried the knife from her hand, and threw it over the side of the mountain. He could see the wound on her temple and blood in her hair and grabbed the sling, tearing it into three pieces. The first he wrapped around the girl's head to bandage the wound, tied the second piece around his leg, and the last to bind up his hand.

The boy sat back in the snow and stared at the young girl, lucky to be alive yet feeling guilt gnawing in his stomach. Exhausted and bleeding from two wounds, he sensed they would both die, if they stayed much longer. He inspected the black diamond. It was truly beautiful, as exquisite in its way as Alius but it represented everything evil on the island. He grabbed the gem with his right hand and pitched it into the blizzard, lost sight of it in the blowing snow, but heard it clatter down the rocks below. "We've got to get out of here, now!"

He struggled to stand on his good leg and leaned over the girl, dragging her to a large boulder, perching her so he could lift her onto his back. "She's tiny. She can't be that heavy," he thought, staggering dangerously close to the edge under the weight. Steadying himself with his injured hand, he began to back down the rock shoot.

It took twice as long to descend from the ledge as it had to climb it and he stumbled several times, sliding and bouncing through a narrow gap between the boulders. Exhausted, he leaned back against a large stone, while he caught his breath in the freezing wind. His strength was sapped and his body wounded and, on his first step, he tumbled backwards down the last ravine of loose rocks to the base of the knot and collapsed to the ground as Alius slipped from his shoulders.

Tic was sitting on the snow, licking his paw, staring at him when he regained consciousness. "It took you long enough! You missed all the fun!" he said, impatiently. "And who's that?"

"That's Alius, the *seer* for the others."

"Oh, she must be the one who hit Brandy with a stone. He's just coming to."

Adrian peered around. The red dog was lying in a heap, just in front of the base of the knot, and he noticed ten or twelve bodies lying in the snow, the second contingent of guards sent to stop him. Most were comatose, some moaning, but all were alive.

"What happened," asked Adrian?

"Another squad of guards but they were no match for our friends. Unfortunately, while we were fighting with them, this one that you just brought down, managed to get past us. Sorry."

Adrian focused on the two hawks and the eagle sitting above him on a large craggy rock. The snakes slithered slowly across the snow, just in front of a large buck, two mountain goats, several rabbits, raccoons, Beggar the bear, and a mountain lion in a circle around him.

"Thank you all," said Adrian. The animals nodded approvingly. The wounded boy crawled over to Brandy and stroked the hair around the wound on his head. "Are you alright?" he asked.

Brandy looked him square in the eyes, "That one is very quick," he said. "I'm embarrassed that she hit me with a rock!"

"Don't be. You slowed her down just enough to allow me to replace the crystal!"

Brandy rolled over and struggled to his feet. "Oh, my head," he groaned, staggering to gain his balance.

"What are you going to do with this one?" asked Tic.

"I think we should take her with us," said Adrian.

"What, are you crazy?"

"No. I'm weak, tired, and beat up...but I'm not crazy," said Adrian. "Without a *seer*, they won't be able to do this again. Besides, we can't take her back to her people, 'oh, by the way, here's your *seer* back'...and we certainly can't leave her here to die."

"I see your point," said Tic, after a moment. "Alright, then. If you are up to it, it's time to get moving. They'll be sending more guards to rescue this bunch."

The large buck stepped up to Adrian, "Put her on my back and tie her on with your scarf. I think I can manage her."

Adrian struggled to his feet and tried to lift the girl. She seemed much heavier now. The eagle and one of the hawks flew over and grabbed the back of her uniform and a mountain goat buried his horns beneath her and pushed. Finally, she drooped across the stag's back and Adrian pulled off his scarf, tying each end to arm and a leg, and looping the rest around the buck's horns, "How's that?"

"Could you push her forward a little? It will help me to balance."

Adrian and the birds grabbed the limp body, pushed her forward, and tightened the lashing, "Better?"

"Yes! Let's get moving."

Tic ran ahead, bouncing and prancing through the snow, as if leading the marching band in a holiday parade, as the procession slowly slogged down the narrow, icy path.

—◦◦◦—

The two men huddled together under blankets inside the trolley, half buried in a drift of snow, and they were as cold as either could remember.

Slowly, the pelting snowfall eased, the wind died down, and a few stars peeked through the clouds. "He's done it!" cried the Professor, hugging George.

They jumped out of the trolley and tramped through thinning flurries to the animal track winding down the rocky face of the mountain. There, not far above, the most unusual squad of warriors that either of them might have imagined straggled through the narrow gap. Tic bounded from rock to rock. Following less gingerly, Adrian leaned on Brandy, but it was not clear who was holding who up, and behind them, a proud and beautiful stag carried a large black lump across his back. Several rabbits, two large goats, and a mountain lion marched out of the darkness, with raccoons, squirrels, and a small bear bringing up the rear. Magnus, the eagle, screeched to announce their arrival and the two hawks carried the snakes very gently in their talons, patrolling in slow circles above the warriors.

As the menagerie reached flat ground, the clouds parted and the first rays of sunrise flooded over the eastern horizon, painting the swirling clouds with streaks of red and amber. George ran through the snow and took Adrian in his arms, "Are you alright? You're bleeding!"

"A bit nicked up but I'll be fine." His eyes were not focusing and his knees were weak.

"What's this?" asked the Professor, pointing at the black bundle on the stag's back.

"That's Alius. She's their *seer*. We couldn't see leaving her up there and it made no sense to allow her to put us through all of this again, so we brought her back to you. You can figure a way to win her over!"

George untied the girl, carried her to the trolley, and wrapped her in blankets. Adrian turned back to the animals, "I couldn't have done this without you. I don't know how to express my thanks."

The stag shook himself off, "We couldn't have accomplished your mission. You saved our way of life, so it is we who should be thanking you."

Adrian stumbled to each of his companions and stroked them, hugged them, and thanked each in turn. He even petted the snakes, which coiled up, hissed, and wiggled their tongues at him in appreciation.

George and Ponte loaded Brandy, Tic, and the snakes into the trolley and Adrian crawled into the back with the animals, turning to the mountain. The knot glowed a fierce crimson against the black rocks and patches of deep blue sky pushed through the clouds. He sighed and closed his eyes.

Sara sputtered, as small waves rolled her body along the edge of the surf, and sat up slowly, coughing, to gaze up and down the white beach. She spied John, lying on his back fifteen or twenty feet away, with his arms covering his face and crawled through the surf to him. "John!" she said softly, "John, can you hear me?"

He groaned and rolled over to face her, "We're alive."

They held each other for a moment, struggled to stand, and slowly staggered up the beach to sprawl on the sand. The storm had passed and The Sparrow was consumed in her wrath but the sun was peaking over the eastern horizon and seagulls swooped through the air, cawing loudly.

From the contours of the beach and the soaring ridge at the spine of the island goring a huge black mountain erupting above a thick blanket of palm trees, one might hope that the bare essentials for survival were available in abundance. Sara and John kissed, as the first rays of sunshine lit up the rocks on the mountain with a bold red

glimmer, its arms reached up, down, east, and west. Bruised and
exhausted, they fell back on the sand.

Chapter Eleven

Two days later, Adrian awoke with a start to find Elsie and the two girls sitting in chairs beside his bed.

"What's happened?" His head throbbed, a searing pain raked his thigh, and his hand was numb beneath a heavy bandage.

"Oh, you're awake. You gave us quite a worry!" said Elsie, rising to wipe his forehead with a cool damp cloth. Molly and Megan jumped up and wrapped their arms around him.

"Oh, we're so proud of you!" said Megan.

"You're our hero!" said Molly, plopping down on the bed next to him.

"I'm no hero," groaned Adrian, "but I think there are a bunch of animals who ought to be thanked too!"

"Well, you saved the island. That makes you a hero!"

"How's Brandy?"

"He'll be fine. I'm sure he's got a headache to match yours but I think he'll recover. He's downstairs," said Elsie, pushing the boy back down into the pillows. "You will stay put! Are you hungry?"

"Yes," said Adrian, suddenly feeling very warm and comfortable. He looked at the curtains, billowing gently at the windows, shimmering in the sunshine.

"I'll bring you something," said Elsie, as she turned to leave the room. "Girls, you make sure he doesn't try to get up and don't bounce around on his bed!"

"Could you bring Brandy and Tic back with you?" asked Adrian.

"Certainly, dear."

The twins tried to contain a bushel of questions but it was no use and they chattered about his achievement and his new status until Elsie returned with a tray. His nurses propped Adrian up on his pillows and slowly ladled sips of warm broth and bites of soggy toast over his blistered lips. Tic jumped up on the bed and sat down at his knees, cocking his head, "Glad to see that you're going to live!"

"I think I've got you to thank for that!" said Adrian, reaching out to rub the cat behind his ears as Brandy limped slowly into the room. He had a bandage around his head with his shaggy red ears hanging out and two more that formed booties on his front legs. "What happened to your paws?"

"Cut them up on the rocks," said Brandy, "but I'll be fine."

Adrian leaned to stroke his soft ears, "I'm sorry that you got hurt."

"That makes two of us. Let's hope we don't have to do that again. Once is enough!"

"What happened to Alius?"

"She's at the Professor's. She came around yesterday and, after protesting loudly for almost twenty-four hours, it seems she's settled in for the time being. She has little choice. In her condition, she can't climb the mountain and, besides, Ester always wanted a daughter of her own, so, this might work out well for everyone until things are more settled," said Elsie.

Adrian finished his soup and toast and drifted into a deep sleep. When he awoke, the curtains hung limp and dark, save the glow of a small fire in the little hearth. George sat transfixed in a chair next to the bed, studying what appeared to be a nautical chart under an amber *orb* that was hanging in midair.

"Ah, you've decided to join us again. Good to see you!"

Adrian groaned and tried to sit up...very slowly, "What time is it?"

"It's getting on for midnight. You've been asleep for quite a while."

His mind was a jumble of flashing memories of wind, snow, and bitter cold, and he struggled to focus his thoughts. He turned to George, "How's the rest of the island?"

"Well, the village is pretty well destroyed. That'll take a while to rebuild. We re-floated one of the sunken trawlers and we'll get the other one in a day or two. The fields were flooded and we've lost a lot of crops...but we'll start again. The Professor says that the vectors are functioning properly and he's busy redesigning the power grid. I assume he intends to avoid having this repeated...ever!"

"What about the *others*?"

"There's been no sign of them but we're prepared to defend the island if we have to."

"And Alius?"

"I think she's a bit confused by her new surroundings but I have a hunch she'll come around, once she realizes that life can be filled with sunshine and the goodness of nature. She's a very strong spirit."

Adrian rubbed the wound on his head with a bandaged hand, "Yeah, I noticed."

George laughed, "I've been thinking...studying the charts. When you recover, what would you think of taking a little journey? We'll have one trawler in good working order shortly and I'm sure that the other two can be repaired before too long. From what your father told me, I understand you're quite a sailor."

The boy stared at his uncle.

He tilted his head and peered over his glasses, "Once things are organized, the other men can handle rebuilding the village and Elsie and the girls can handle the farm. I think it might be time to go looking for your parents."

"Are you kidding?"

"No, son, I'm not. I just don't believe they're dead. Your father was a man of the sea and I think they're out there somewhere. If they are, we'll find them."

Adrian settled back into his pillows. This was going to be the fastest recovery in history.

Adrian's aunt bustled into the room and placed a tray on a bed stand. She smiled but her blue eyes could not conceal her concern, "Here's your breakfast, dear."

"Thank you," said Adrian, pushing himself up on his pillows. He had been confined to bed since his battle on the mountain and he was ready to get up. The sun was shining through his window and he longed to be outside, to smell the salt air and feel the wind on his face.

"Dr. Stevens will be here shortly to check your wounds," said Elsie. "You've been a good patient and I know you're ready to get up, but let's see what the doctor has to say."

"Alright," said Adrian quietly. He picked up his toast and began to eat. Fresh apple juice, two eggs, a small piece of fried fish, and fresh fruit covered the plate. Elsie had arranged a few small roses in a tiny vase on his tray and Adrian picked up the urn and inhaled the sweet scent, which made him even more anxious to escape his prison.

He looked up at his aunt, "I have a question."

"Yes, dear?"

"The portraits in the parlor...are they our relatives? I know about my grandparents on my father's side but my mother never spoke about your parents."

Elsie's lips curled into a small sad smile and she sat, gently, on the edge of the bed, "Yes, they are. The woman on the right is your grandmother, Alison, who died during childbirth when your mother was born. The man is your grandfather, Paul, who disappeared a few weeks after your grandmother died. Some said that he couldn't bear the anguish of losing his wife, others said that, in his rage, he set out on a quest to conquer the secrets of the dark powers. Whatever his reasons or whatever he found, he never came back."

"And the other woman?"

"Her name was Mazie and she moved into this house and raised the two of us as if we were her own daughters. She never married and died when I was seventeen. If we could have picked our mother at birth, she would have been our first choice and we owe who we have become to her love and kindness."

"As to why your mother never speaks of our parents, it's because she only knew them second hand, through family stories and the memories of others. She never had real parents of her own and, perhaps, that's why she works so hard at being a good parent to you."

"Is that why she never told me about my...heritage?"

Elsie stared into his eyes for a long moment, "I think that the thought of you inheriting the gifts of a *seer* frightened her. After all...in spite of the wonders of the Crystals, the father that she never knew abandoned his newborn daughter, consumed by the temptation or, perhaps, the redemption of the dark powers. For her, it was all tangled together in the one thing that she could never have... and, knowing my sister, the fact that she never spoke of it was her way of protecting you." She smiled sadly, kissed his forehead, and left the room.

Molly and Megan burst through the door and jumped on the edge of his bed. "How are you feeling?" inquired Molly, grabbing a piece of toast from his tray.

Adrian slapped her hand and laughed, "I'm feeling fine and I'm ready to get out of this bed!"

"We're ready too!" giggled Megan. "Morgan has come by every day to see you but Mother won't let her come up. Ian, Kelly, and Joshua came by yesterday."

"Why not?"

"She's decided that you can't have any visitors until the Doctor gives his approval. She's just being a mom."

Adrian cleared his plate, with a little help from the girls, "I want to go back to the forest to thank our friends for their help."

"We'll take you as soon as you get your bones out of this bed," said Megan.

Elsie marched through the door to retrieve the tray, followed by Dr. Stevens, and ushered the girls out of the room, leaving Adrian alone with the doctor. He was a very tall, slender man, with spectacles sitting low on the bridge of a narrow nose beneath dark hallow eyes above boney cheekbones. Salt and pepper hair reached well below his collar in the back, and a thick gray mustache curled up at the ends like the horns of a mountain goat. Graceful fingers withdrew an ancient gold pocket watch, suspended on a chain across his vest, to take Adrian's pulse. He touched Adrian's forehead, to check for a fever, and then took a small scope out of his little black bag. He aimed a small beam into Adrian's eyes, moving back and forth in front of Adrian's face, "You're looking better. How do you feel?"

"My headache is better and the gashes have stopped throbbing. I'm ready to get out of this bed!"

"Well, let's have a look at those wounds and we'll see," said Dr. Stevens, as he reached into his bag and withdrew a pair of scissors. He snipped the bandages from Adrian's hand and then his leg and inspected the lacerations, "These are healing nicely, there doesn't seem to be any infection and the stitches are holding up." He checked the bruise above his eye and then the gash behind his left ear, humming approvingly, "I've brought you a pair of crutches and I'll make you a deal. If you will promise to take it easy, you can get up and start moving around."

"Can I go outside?"

"Yes, but no running around. I don't want you to reopen your wounds. Do we have a deal?"

"You bet!" said Adrian, swinging his legs over the side of the bed.

"Not so fast. I want to clean your wounds with my healing waters and then you can get up."

Adrian held up his hand to be bandaged and then offered his leg. He could hardly restrain the anticipation of a reprieve from the confines of his shrinking room.

"I've just been to see Alius," said the Doctor.

"How is she?"

"She's better. She still has a headache but she'll be all right. You must have hit her pretty hard."

"She was trying to carve me up, I had no other choice," replied the boy with a hint of guilt.

"What did you hit her with?"

Adrian looked down at the wrappings that the Doctor had secured, "A giant black diamond."

The doctor laughed gently, "There's an irony there but you're lucky you didn't break her skull!"

Adrian felt embarrassed. He had been taught that you do not hit girls under any circumstances…but no one ever told him what to do with a girl who was wielding a knife, with murder in her eyes.

"She wants to see you," said the doctor gently.

"I'd like that, as long as she doesn't have a knife!" smiled Adrian.

"I'll ask Elsie to talk with Ester," said Dr. Stevens, "perhaps they can set it up for tomorrow. In the meantime, let's see how you do with your crutches today. If you have any throbbing in your wounds or if your head begins to hurt or your eyes don't focus or you get dizzy or nauseous, I want you back into bed and have Elsie call me immediately. Do you promise?"

"Yes sir!" said Adrian, swinging his legs out of bed. He put his good foot on the floor, as Dr. Stevens brought the crutches to him. He felt light-headed for a moment but nothing was going to stop him from escaping these four walls as soon as possible. A pile of clean clothes laid out on the chair in his room had been taunting him for several days and he could not wait to put them on.

"I'll be back tomorrow to check on you," said Dr. Stevens. "Remember, we have a deal. You will take it easy?"

"Yes, sir, and thank you!"

The door opened as the Doctor left and Adrian peeled off his nightshirt, pulling his pants gingerly over his wound. It was sore and he did not want anything to slow down his recovery. He wiggled into a shirt and found that the knot on his head throbbed when he leaned over to put on socks and shoes. He stood on his good leg and picked up the crutches.

The door groaned open as he hobbled across the room, "It's nice to see you up and about!"

"Thank you," said Adrian.

The girls were waiting in the hallway and helped him down the stairs and into the kitchen, where Elsie was busy at the sink. "Oh, it's so nice to see you up!"

"It's nice to be up," said Adrian, "and thank you for taking care of me."

"It is we who should thank you. The other children have been by to see you but I wouldn't let them bother you until the Doctor said it was alright. Almost every adult on the island has called on the *messenger* to check up on you. You've managed to win a place in everyone's heart."

"I just did what had to be done, nothing more," said Adrian, with an embarrassed blush.

"Dr. Stevens said that you've agreed to see Alius?" inquired Elsie, with a twinkle in her eye. "That is very big of you, considering everything. I'll call Ester this afternoon and arrange it for tomorrow, if you're feeling up to it?"

"Yes, I'd like that. Thank you."

The young *seer* thumped his way to the back door. Balancing on crutches was going to take a little getting used to and he found that his left hand hurt when he reached to grasp the banister. The twins guided him down the steps. It seemed a very long time ago that he and his mother sat here in the darkness, before his parents sailed away on the Sparrow, and he was no longer that boy. At times, during his delirium, he could hear their voices echoing from a great distance and something deep in his soul knew they were alive. He was anxious to talk with George about when they could get started on a journey to find them.

Adrian stopped at the bottom of the stairs and turned to face the sun. He tilted his head back and closed his eyes, absorbing the warmth on his face, refreshing after being cooped up in his room, and inhaled the thick rich salt air blowing in from the ocean.

They walked slowly into the garden. The vegetables had suffered from the cold and the storm but there were vibrant green buds showing here and there. Small flowers, bursting from new growth above brown bedraggled leaves, offered themselves up to bees and butterflies moving between the plants carting pollen from one bud to the next. Adrian turned to the south where the fields of crops looked trampled by an enormous creature in some bizarre dance that left random patches untouched between wide swaths that were completely flattened.

Several goats and two cows wandered over to Adrian and the girls. "We're glad to see that you are better," said one of the goats.

"Thank you," said Adrian, reaching his good hand to pet the goat's ear. "It's nice to be outside."

Adrian turned to look back at the house. On his arrival, it was simply his aunt and uncle's charming, though desolate, farmhouse, a place where he would be held in comfortable and somewhat magical oblivion for a couple of months…but now it seemed a very special house, a home. Several of the trees had broken branches, suffered during the storm, but the house itself seemed to have survived without damage. The slate roof hung at a steep angle over two stories of solid gray stone and all the windows opened to a warm gentle breeze from the southeast. Patches of ivy crawled up the walls almost to the roofline and the shutters, flanking each window, were painted a bright aqua that was complimented by masses of yellow flowers erupting in clusters from shrubs planted around the foundation. Adrian felt as if he was seeing the house for the first time and he loved it.

George was standing on the roof of the barn, sawing a large limb into pieces that tumbled into a pile on the ground. He waved to the children and yelled, "It's nice to see you up and about!"

Over his uncle's shoulder, Adrian spied a large black bird flying high over the ridge, soaring on the thermals. He was reminded of the huge black ravens over the bay at home but he could not be sure whether this was one of those. He was distracted by a small wagon rolling into the yard. Morgan, Joshua, Ian, and Kelly jumped out and ran over to Adrian and the girls. Morgan gave Adrian a big hug and Kelly latched on to his good leg.

"We're so glad to see you," said Joshua, smiling. "How are you feeling?"

"I'll be alright," said Adrian. "The Doctor says that I'm healing nicely."

"We're all so proud of you! We wish that we could have helped," said Morgan, draping a long slender arm around his shoulder.

"I had some very good help from the animals. I couldn't have done it without them."

"We want to hear the story," said Ian, who seemed a little bit sullen, standing at the back of the group.

The children moved to some split log benches near the kitchen door. Morgan sat very close to Adrian and he noticed that her mouth smiled without concealing the concern in her eyes. He briefly recounted his adventure, not wanting to sound boastful or a martyr, and ended by saying, "There is nothing that I did that any of you wouldn't have done."

Morgan replied, "I'm not sure that any of us would have known what to do, let alone been brave enough to try."

"Yes, you would," replied Adrian, staring at Ian. "It was just that there was no other choice."

"She's right, you know," said Ian. "We might have been brave enough, or stupid enough to try, but you figured out what to do. None of us could have done that part."

Adrian looked up at his second cousin, "I didn't volunteer for any of this and I certainly didn't have a clue what I was getting into but, once you or I or any of us commit to doing what's right, there's no turning back. That's what makes this island and our people so special, they're defending what's right and true."

Elsie brought juice and cookies for the children, who sat and talked into the afternoon. Adrian felt accepted or, perhaps, honored by his new friends and he could not help rejoicing, in spite of the pain of his wounds and fears about his parents.

Chapter Twelve

The five Masters sat at the round table under the purple glow of an *orb* in the snarl of grotesque gargoyles writhing in the cove of the ceiling. Mandor and Nanchez stood silently before the council. Nanchez suffered a burn from a small explosion in the lab when the circuits switched over and Mandor had stitches to seal the wounds around his eyes.

"Your plan failed completely," exclaimed Jofre, who was seated at the center of the Council. His voice was deep and gravelly, a menacing torrent thrashing around the night creatures peering down through the darkness of the dome. Mandor and Nanchez stared at their feet to avoid the intensity in his white eyes. "How could this happen?" he shouted.

"Master, we were overwhelmed," replied Mandor quietly.

"You had weapons!"

"None of our men ever confronted such an onslaught of creatures. There were mountain lions, large deer, bears, hawks, eagles, and poisonous snakes. Several of our men were seriously wounded and a dozen are still in the infirmary suffering from the venom of the snakes, animal bites, lacerations, and broken bones. We were unprepared."

"We will not be unprepared again, will we?"

"No sir," said the two men quietly.

"Are the systems functioning properly?"

"Yes, Master," replied Nanchez. "We had a back flow that incinerated our tracking circuits and most of the lab, but we'll have them back up in no time."

"They've taken our *seer* and I will have her back!" screamed The Master. "I want a plan to retrieve her and I will have it by tomorrow morning! Must I ask for volunteers?"

"No, Master."

The two men snapped, painfully, to attention and bowed.

"Place a team of observers with a scope at the mouth of the tunnel to scour the south side of the island, I want to know where they're holding her and whether they are massing for a counter-attack. We will expect you in these chambers at dawn tomorrow to review your plan! Once we have recovered her, we'll consider an invasion. You are excused."

"Yes, Master." The two men turned and marched to the entrance. The small woman unlatched the door and followed them out. She turned, twisted the key in the lock, and resumed her post, as the two men shuffled down the hallway. Only the chafing of their leather uniforms and the uneven cadence of their heavy boots broke the hum of the machinery. Neither spoke, for each was absorbed in the orders that they had just received…and the consequences of failure.

After breakfast, the girls helped Adrian into the back of the wagon and Megan took the wheel, turning onto the north path. Adrian was reminded of the last time he traversed this trail when the storm was howling and the path coated with slick ice. The trolley bounced from side to side, like the bumper cars at the festival gone crazy.

He gazed up at the black mountain with just a twinge of snow at the peak, so tame and serene, compared to the tempestuous darkness a few days ago. His spine tingled with that familiar chill and his whole body shivered.

Ester and the Professor walked up to the wagon, as they pulled into the path to the observatory. "We're so glad to see you. We've been worried about you!" cried Ester. Ponte waddled around the wagon and helped Adrian climb out the back. The girls handed his crutches down as Tic jumped out of the bed and rubbed up against Ester's leg. She leaned over, hoisted the huge cat into her arms, and squeezed him tightly.

"How's Alius?" asked Adrian.

"She's a bit confused but she's anxious to see you," said Professor Ponte.

Adrian turned to the girls and said, "I think I ought to speak with her alone and then I'll introduce you, if you're alright with that?"

"Sure," said Molly.

"She's around back, sitting in the sun," said Ester, her thin lips stretched over her too small teeth in an affectionate smile, "and...we are all so very proud of you." She seemed softer, less stern.

Adrian blushed his most bashful smile and hobbled away around the house beneath the stone pillar. He looked up to a glint on the curve of the dome, gleaming in the bright sunshine. Alius was sitting on the grass, leaning back on her elbows with her head tilted to catch the warmth. She wore a bandage that formed a cap, with her white hair poking out beneath the bottom of the wrap, shorts and a tee shirt, that were much too large, and her pale skin showed more than a faint blush of color. She seemed smaller and more slender than she had in her uniform and cloak during their battle on the mountain but the muscles in her arms and legs were taut and well defined. She gazed up at him curiously, as he approached. "How are you?" she asked, with what seemed genuine concern. Her electric blue eyes flashed in the sunlight.

"I'll mend. How about you?"

"I've still got a terrific headache, but Dr. Stevens says it will get better over time."

"I'm sorry I hit you so hard."

"I know. Me too. Will you sit with me?"

"Yes, I'd like that," said Adrian, slowly lowering himself onto her blanket, placing the crutches on the ground. They stared at each other. Adrian felt as if he had known her forever and yet they had shared but a few moments, a few words, and a deadly struggle, "How's life with the Professor and Ester?"

"I miss my...my life...but they are very kind. The Professor's so incredibly smart and his sense of humor is kind of crazy. Ester is a bit stern but she is so concerned with my well being, that I can't really hold it against her. I guess I should thank you for bringing me down from the mountain."

"I couldn't leave you there, you would have died...and I couldn't very well have taken you back to your people, 'oh, hi...sorry to bother you but here's your *seer.*' So there really wasn't much choice."

"Well, thank you. I doubt anyone would have blamed you, if you hadn't."

They were quiet for a while, sitting on the grass. Finally, Alius said, "Do you know this is the first time in my life that I've been able to sit in the sunshine? Sure the sun comes around the mountain when we near the solstice and I've been out on the trawlers a few times but my world is shadows and tunnels."

Adrian smiled, gazing across the fields and the dense green forest running the length of the island along the ridge. "It is lovely, isn't it?"

"Yes," she said quietly. "I'm afraid that I'm a bit confused by all of this. I've been thinking about what you said, during our fight on the mountain. You said that it might be our destiny to stand in the sunlight but it was not our right."

"Yes, I did say that."

"You also said that the people who live on the south side of the island have worked for generations to build a paradise and I can see what you mean, as I look out over the island. It's so lush and green. There are trees everywhere and the fields are overflowing with crops. The few people that I've met seem to smile a lot. They enjoy life here. Where I come from, life is a struggle...every day is filled with duty...and survival."

"I'm new to this island. I grew up on the mainland, so I'm just learning about this way of life too. There's a lot that I've yet to understand about this place and these people, but I know that they're good and kind, that they work very hard, and they believe in a balance between man and nature. That's part of the reason they've been so successful."

"Then how can you be a *seer*?"

"My mother was born here," replied Adrian.

Alius looked into Adrian's eyes, "We have the same eyes, could it be that we're related?"

"I honestly don't know. I guess it's possible. I've only heard a vague story about your people migrating to the other side of the mountain many generations ago."

"I was raised to believe in my own people, in our history, our customs, and our way of life, but I can see things here that could never exist on the north side of the island. We were taught that the people of the south island betrayed and banished our ancestors to the cold of the mountain so they could keep the golden powers for themselves. You were the enemy that all of us could hate together. The threat, that your friends and family posed, provided the excuse for our regimented and disciplined life." She was quiet for a moment. A tear rolled down her cheek, "I'm so confused. Part of me wants to run back to home to the security of my life as I know it, and, at the same time, I want to know more about life here on the south side of the island. It's almost as if my whole world is based on a lie."

"I wish I knew the answer but I'd like to introduce you to some of the things that I've learned about these wonderful people. Perhaps understanding what they believe will provide a different perspective. My cousins take me to a very special place to picnic in the forest. Would you like to come with us? I think it would help you to see the magic of this place."

"I'd like that."

Adrian stared at the beautiful *seer*, her brilliant blue eyes mirrored his own but there was a coldness hidden there. Her nose was small and very straight. She had high cheekbones and full lips that struggled to yield a smile over perfect white teeth. Long slender fingers extended from expressive hands that seemed to dance in the air around her face.

"I have a question…we're both *seers*, yet you said that you were brought up on the mainland. How did you learn that you were a *seer*?" she asked in a quiet voice.

"When the storm came up, my uncle George asked if I would be willing to read from the Book of Wisdoms because none of the adults or the other children inherited the gift. When did you know that you were one?"

"I guess I've always known. My father is the most powerful man in our world and, when I was very young, he placed a black diamond pendant around my neck, took me to a cavern deep in the mountain, and asked me to look at a strange silver book. He called it the Book of Knowledge. It made sense to me from the first moment I watched the crazy figures wander around the pages. I could ask questions and it would answer.

Once my father realized I was a *seer*, I was required to study the book almost every day. I attended classes with the other children but, after school, they'd go off to play and I'd disappear into a secluded room to study The Book. I felt different. I'm sure the other children never knew what I was doing but it was a secret that provided my classmates an excuse to ostracize me."

"That must have been hard on you," said Adrian, noticing that when she spoke of her home, her hands clenched into fists.

"I never felt that I fit in with the other children because I was trained to serve The Council. I was taught that honoring that calling is…or was the purpose of my life. I always wondered what it would be like to be a normal child. I still wonder." Alius was staring at an ant crawling up a blade of grass. Tears flowed, as she sobbed quietly, "I'm so confused."

Adrian reached over and gently touched her arm, "I think I understand some of what you're saying. This is all new to me. I never suspected that I had any weird talents and I certainly never expected to be in the position of having to fight for the survival of these very special people that I hardly knew. I guess I just realized that this is a magical place, a place that should be the model for life on the rest of this planet. Nothing should be allowed to change or disrupt what they've created."

They were quiet for a while. Alius sobbed silently, long fingers clenched into a fist at her lips.

"Have you met Tic the cat?" asked Adrian, hoping to brighten the moment.

"He's quite a character. I've never had a conversation with an animal before. That was a very strange experience." Alius wiped her eyes on the sleeves of her too large shirt and grinned. "He's been back and forth to check on you."

"All of the animals talk with each other and with the people on this side of the island. They saved my life and helped to save yours. That's part of what they call The Balance."

Adrian noticed that Alius' nose was beginning to turn red, "Perhaps we ought to go in. You are starting to get a sunburn."

"I've never had a sunburn," replied Alius.

"You don't want one, promise. They hurt!"

"Let's go in then."

"I want to introduce you to my cousins, Molly and Megan. They're twins, identical twins. Molly talks fast and looks directly into your eyes. Megan's a little more laid back but they're both funny."

Alius rose very slowly, holding her head level and steady. She reached out her right hand and helped Adrian up, picked up his crutches, and gathered her things. They walked around the tower and into the house.

Ester was waiting at the door and put her arm around Alius. Adrian could feel the bond developing and Ester's manner revealed how much she cared for her new charge. As Alius looked up at her surrogate mother, Adrian saw a flash of tenderness in her eyes that he had not seen before. The old woman guided them into the parlor, "Come along you two, you'll enjoy this."

Molly and Megan were playing three-dimensional chess over the table in front of the fireplace. The pieces floated from one space to another within a shimmering grid that hovered between them. Tic sat on the arm of Molly's chair, instructing her on the impending move. "You don't know how to play chess, Tic!" cried Molly.

"True," said Tic, stoically, "but I do understand strategy. I proved that on the mountain!"

The girls turned, as Adrian and Alius hobbled into the room. Adrian introduced Alius, "Molly and Megan, I'd like you to meet Alius."

Molly and Megan both stood and scurried over to greet them. "How's your head?" asked Megan. "From what Adrian said, you two had quite a tussle on the mountain."

Molly took Alius by the arm and led her to the chess game they were playing, "Come join us. Do you play?"

"I've played regular chess on a board but I'm afraid I've never seen anything like this," she said, staring at the floating frame and the pieces scattered within.

"It's another of the Professor's games. He's so inventive," laughed Megan. "He said that he has a surprise for us today."

As if on queue, Ponte emerged from the elevator with a small shiny object in his hands. "Ah, you've come just in time. You'll all like this one! I call it a three-dimensional gyroscope."

The Professor held out his hand for the children to inspect his latest invention. It had three shiny silver wheels intersecting at the center, surrounding a small blue crystal that glowed dimly. "Normal gyroscopes only work in two dimensions. You can spin them up, put them on a surface, and they'll wander about as they spin…but this one works in three dimensions. Watch!"

He held the shiny toy in the palm of his hand and pulled a short string sharply. The three wheels began to spin rapidly and the faint glow within the crystal blazed. He balanced the gyroscope on the tip of his finger then pulled away. The spinning gyroscope floated in mid-air, rotating around a small circle. The children all giggled in amazement.

Alius reached out a finger and gently touched the spinning toy. It moved to one side and righted itself. "Oh, that's wonderful!"

The Professor reached up, took it out of the air, and handed it to Alius. "I thought you'd like it. Please accept it as a gift. The rest of you will just have to wait until I've a chance to make more of them!"

Alius took it, carefully, and held it up in the palm of her hand. The Professor showed her how to rig the little string. She pulled it, then balanced the toy on her fingertip and slowly released it to hang in the air. All of the children were entranced and took turns spinning it up.

Alius turned to the Professor, "Thank you. I'm not sure that I've ever received a gift that was so much fun!"

"You're welcome, my dear. Enjoy it," smiled the Professor, turning to the cages where the birds were kept. "Now we have some serious work to do. Magnus, our fallen eagle, proved the other night that his wounds have healed sufficiently. It is time for him to fly."

Adrian walked over to the cage and greeted the two hawks, Harry and Harriet, and the eagle, who had fought for him on the mountain, "I'm glad all of you are better and I want to thank you for your help."

"We only wish that we could have done more," said Magnus, "all I could do was fly cover for my friends here."

"It was perfect, everyone had a role," said Adrian. "Come on Alius, they won't hurt you."

Alius held back, unsure of these powerful creatures. Ester gently pushed her forward and she approached the cages with more than a bit of hesitation. Adrian took her hand to stroke the eagle. "Your feathers are so soft, yet strong,"

"The better to fly with," squawked the eagle.

"Alius, would you like to set Magnus free?" asked the Professor. He had a long, thick glove, which he handed to Alius. "Put this on your right arm. I have one on my left and I'll carry him outside. Then you can take him and let him fly."

Alius could not contain her smile and pushed her hand into the glove, as the Professor stepped up to the cage and reached inside. Magnus stepped off the perch and onto the Professor's arm, and the group walked slowly out the door and into the sunshine across the path.

The professor held his arm out straight, next to Alius, and Magnus stepped onto Alius' glove. He was heavy and Alius had to use both hands to hold him at eye level. The eagle squawked and fluttered his huge wings. Alius pinched her eyes closed, as the giant bird pressed his beak against her nose, and she broke into a dazzling smile.

There was a short string hooked to a clip on Magnus' leg. The professor handed the string to Alius and said, "When you two are ready, I'll detach the clip. Magnus you are free to go, but please come back to visit on a regular basis."

Molly, Megan, and Adrian stepped closer and each reached out to touch the magnificent king of the sky. Alius was captivated by the beautiful creature. She never had a pet and certainly never held a full-grown eagle, so she was a bit reluctant to end this very special moment. The eagle looked down into her eyes, "I've learned to avoid your side of the island. That is where I got shot with a pellet from a sling…but I will always look for you, for you are the one who set me free."

"I'm sorry that you got shot but I'm honored to be the one to put you back in the air where you belong," said Alius. She held up her arm and the Professor unlatched the clip on Magnus' shin.

The eagle fluttered his wings a few times, as if to test their strength, "They seem to be working. Thank you, Professor, for taking such good care of me. I am in your debt." With that, he stretched out his great wings, scooped up the air, and flew slowly across the field next to the observatory with long graceful thrusts. He gained speed and altitude with each stroke until he was a golden speck flying out over the bluffs to the ocean.

The children cheered and the Professor looked so very proud. He put his gloved arm around Alius' shoulders and smiled, "My dear, that is The Balance and now you are a part of it."

Alius beamed, "I think that I'm beginning to understand…and thank you for letting me be the one."

"I wouldn't have it any other way. Now children, I'm sure that we can find more amusements in the parlor but let's see if Miss Ester can conjure up something for us to nibble on." The Professor and Ester herded the children back into the stone house beneath the column of black rock and the door closed behind them.

Chapter Thirteen

At dawn the following morning, Mandor and Nanchez stood before the large metal doors. The small woman turned the key and ushered them into the sacrosanct Council.

The five Masters sat behind the round table staring at the two giant men in silence. Purple light falling from the ceiling cast eerie shadows on the faces of the Governors. Finally, Jofre inquired, "What has the observer seen?"

"We believe that she is being held at the observatory. She was seen outside yesterday afternoon. Our guards report that she had an eagle on her arm and let it fly!" reported Mandor.

"An eagle?" mused the white-eyed Master.

"Yes, sir!"

"And what of your plan?"

"Sir, there is nothing between the mountain and the observatory. We believe that a mission could be mounted to rush the observatory to retrieve her. We would like to attempt this mission today."

"Have they posted guards?"

"None have been observed, Sir!" said Nanchez. "They seem to be repairing the damage and going about life as normal."

"So, you're recommending a surprise attack?"

"Yes, Sir!"

"How many men do you plan to take with you?"

"A squad of eight, more might draw attention. Our plan is to rush the house at the base of the observatory, retrieve our *seer*, and return before anyone can react," said Mandor, gaining confidence in the plan. "It seems the success of their mysterious *seer* has lulled them into complacence."

"Certainly, they know that we have no *seer* to guide us," said Jofre quietly. "What of the animals?"

"There are animals all over the south side of the island but we have seen no organized defense, Master."

"Then proceed…but do not fail and do not allow anything to happen to our *seer*. Bring her to me on your return. You are excused and we will await your success!"

"Yes, Master," said the two men in unison. They bowed, turned, and exited, followed by the small woman, who again locked the doors and blocked the entry.

Adrian squinted his eyes against the glare of the sun streaming through the window. He rolled out of bed and slowly pulled his pants over his wounded leg, slipped on his shirt, and then socks and shoes. He noticed that his head did not punish him for the effort and his wounds itched. He grabbed his crutches and headed out the door, which creaked as it opened, "Are we feeling better today?"

"Yes, thank you," replied Adrian. The dry humor of the talking door still unnerved him. He balanced the *orb* on the handle of the crutch, thumped down the stairs, and turned into the kitchen to find Elsie just serving breakfast to George and the girls at the oval table. "Good morning everyone!"

"Good morning," said the twins in unison, giggling.

"How are you feeling today?" asked Elsie.

"Much better, thank you. My headache is gone and my gashes seem to be healing." Adrian sat down and turned to his uncle George, "Have you given any thought to beginning the search for my parents?"

"I went down and checked with Travis about the trawlers yesterday. We've managed to re-float the two that went down in the storm and the third seems to be running fine. We did find that the storage tanks are contaminated with water, so we'll have to take the good trawler to the mainland to bring back some clean fuel. One of them has electrical problems too. I think we could probably get started in the next week or two. We want to have at least one of the other trawlers back in commission before we leave and two'd be better."

"I was looking at the maps in my geography book, last night, and I remembered something I learned while I was inside The Crystal last week. It showed where the other Crystals are located all over the planet and I remember seeing one in the area where my parents might have been when The Sparrow was lost. Do you think it's possible that they're stranded on an island?"

"I don't know but perhaps the Professor would let us take a look at the Book of Wisdoms. It would certainly be a good place to start! He's bringing Alius over this morning so all of you can go on a picnic in the forest. We'll ask him when he arrives," said George between bites of toast and eggs.

Adrian smiled, anxious to begin, and felt, in his heart, that his parents were alive because something...an intuition perhaps...was drawing him to an island off the Pacific coast of Mexico.

After breakfast, the children washed the dishes and started to put them away, when an incredible honking erupted in the yard outside that sounded like an invasion of enormous geese gone mad. Adrian grabbed his crutches and hobbled after the twins, as they rushed out the back door to find the Professor behind the wheel of the most fantastic vehicle on the island.

It was bright red, with a little roof over the cab that was trimmed with flaming yellow fringe blowing this way and that in the cool morning breeze. A large cloud of dust was just drifting away and skid marks arced across the path behind the trolley. The Professor and Alius sat in two overstuffed wing chairs that were fastened in the cab just behind twin oval windshields that curved around the sides, creating the illusion that they were melting from speed. A rack of *orbs* stretched across the front of the trolley flashing different colors in some random, crazy pattern, while Alius mashed the bulb of a large brass horn attached to the side of the vehicle, making the most awful racket. They were both laughing hysterically.

"Oh, Professor, this is so much fun," screamed Alius, honking the horn again and again.

"I'm glad you've enjoyed our little ride…the best part is that I'll be back later to pick you up and we can do it again!" They rolled out of the strange trolley and dusted themselves off.

George and Elsie walked over from the barn to exchange hugs and laughter. "We're glad that you made it here safely, Alius. I know how the Professor drives," laughed George.

"It was an adventure. We don't have anything that's this much fun on the other side of the island," said Alius. She wore a smaller bandage on her head and her straight white hair shimmered in the sunshine. There was a faint hint of tan across her nose and cheeks beneath sparkling blue eyes. She was dressed in an old blue shirt and pants that belonged to Ester with legs and sleeves rolled up into loose donuts.

Elsie inspected the child and turned to Molly and Megan, "Why don't you take Alius upstairs and find some clothes that fit her. You two have plenty of things you're not wearing that would do nicely."

Molly and Megan escorted Alius into the house followed by George tending the Professor up the back steps to the kitchen and a seat at the oval table.

"Adrian's come up with some good ideas on finding Sara and John. Tell him what you saw, Adrian," said George.

"While I was in The Crystal, the other day, it showed a map of the world. At first, it only showed one giant continent…I think it was called Pangaea, anyway, gradually, it split into pieces that morphed into the continents as we know them. It also showed where all of the Crystals were originally located and, one by one, many disappeared as the geography changed. The voice told me that many of those were places where the powers were misused, but, if I remember correctly, there was a pair off the west coast of Mexico and I was wondering whether that might be a clue to where my parents landed?"

Professor Ponte pondered this thought for a moment and his lips curled into a small smile, "I certainly don't claim to understand everything about the Crystals and their powers but I do know that they work in mysterious ways. If nothing else, that would be a good place to start the search."

"Could we work with the Book of Wisdoms to see what it has to say?" asked Adrian, anxiously.

"Certainly, my boy. You could come back with me tonight, when I return to pick up Alius, if you like."

"You bet!"

"Right, it's settled then. In the meantime, take good care of our guest. She still has her headache and doesn't need to be running around. I trust that you'll look after her?"

"Yes, sir," smiled Adrian, leaning on his crutches, "I don't think I'll be doing any running for a few days myself."

The girls rushed into the kitchen in a frazzle of giggles with Alius wearing blue jeans and a bright red shirt that was only a little too large compared to Ester's clothes. She was chattering comfortably with the girls, who carried several other outfits for her to wear, as if they'd always known each other.

"Would you take these back with you, Professor?" said Megan, "Alius can use more than one set of clothes and we're happy to share."

"That's very kind of you, girls," said Ponte, smiling brightly. "You look lovely Alius! Did you thank the girls?"

"Oh, yes. They've been so kind."

"Good. Then, I guess I'll be off. I'll come back later this afternoon to pick you up, if that's alright with everyone?"

The group followed the Professor out to his very strange transport. He hopped into the driver's seat and reached over to honk the horn. Everyone covered their ears and laughed. He turned the wheel, spun around, and raced out the gate to the path to the village followed by a whirling cloud of dust.

Elsie led the parade back into the kitchen, "Girls, get one of the baskets from the larder. I've made sandwiches and drinks, and I've got some corn, nuts, and cookies for your friends in the forest."

Megan walked into the pantry, took down a large wicker basket, and returned it to her mother, who carefully filled it with food and drinks and handed it back to them. "Off you go, then. Have a great time but be back well before dinner. Your chores will be waiting."

Adrian thumped after the three girls out the kitchen door and over to the barn. They placed the basket in the back of the wagon and Molly jumped behind the wheel. "My turn to drive!"

"No, it's mine," protested Megan.

George put his arm around Elsie's waist, as they waved to the children. The wagon slowly pulled out of the gate and headed south. "She seems a nice girl," said Elsie.

"Yes, she does…but there's more to her than she's revealing. I'll be interested to see how this plays out," replied George. They turned back into the house as the wagon disappeared over the small hill.

Magnus soared with the thermals, circling north high above the beaches, where he could see beyond the forest on the ridge to the west coast and south over the fields past the crescent beach where the children played.

The sun was perched high in the east and he was searching for a run of fish or a careless rabbit running through the pastures. Here and there, narrow paths burrowed beneath arbors of trees that intersected the fields between the stone houses and, as he flew near the House of Four Seasons, he noticed the Professor's red trolley rolling into the yard in a cloud of dust. He was grateful for the little man's wisdom and kindness. He rolled to his right and arced up the eastern coast.

The fish were not schooling on this side of the island, so he banked to the west well shy of the black mountain. After his injury, he learned to avoid the hunters, so he swept across the fields and spied eight figures in black uniforms running south along the path from the mountain. He tucked his wings and dove within a few feet of the hoods of their cloaks, just as the squad approached the observatory. He circled around the crooked column of rock, feeling helpless to defend his friends, as the troops barged into the front door of the house. After a few minutes, they reappeared, except now there were eight black figures and another dressed in a long blue dress. It was Ester!

He folded his wings close to his body, a predator on the attack, screeching as loud as he could, hoping to break up the formation, but two of the invaders took up kneeling positions and fired, barely missing his newly healed wing. He swung to his right and climbed back into the safety of the air. "I need to find some help!"

He flew west to the forest and then south along the ridgeline, searching the ground for an ally.

Ponte left the House of the Four Seasons and headed to the village to inspect the reconstruction. The giant oak tree lost several massive limbs, which were being sawed into rounds with a two-man saw and piled on the ground. The frontage of the little village suffered considerable damage and several men were working on the roof of the fishmonger's shop, replacing the shingles blown away in the gale. He pulled his red trolley up to the quay and found Travis, the harbormaster, on the deck of one of the boats that had been brought up from the bottom.

"Morning, Professor! This one's a real mess. It'll take a couple of weeks to get her running again. Hull seems to be in good shape but the water has seeped into her engines and corroded the electrical system."

"Good morning to you, Travis. How's the other one?"

"She's coming along. Engines seem alright but she has electrical problems too. We need to make a run to the mainland for some fresh fuel to flush the lines and some spare parts, then we'll know a bit more."

"How's the power in the buildings? I've been working on the grid and it should be back in working order."

Travis took off his hat and rubbed the sweat from his brow with his sleeve, "We've full power but we had to shut down the funhouse and all the storefronts on the north side, circuits shorting out all over the place. We don't need a fire on top of all the damage we're trying to clear out before we can begin repairs but we'll figure it out."

"Good, good," said the Professor. "Is there anything that I can help with here?"

"We can probably use your help with the circuitry, but I want my helpers to get the roof patched before we get to that. How about coming around this afternoon and we'll take a look?"

"Right you are, I'll be back after lunch. Anything that you need?"

"Bring some of your fuses, switches, and we could probably use more *orbs* to light up the inside. We should have plenty of cable."

"I'll be back in a few hours with the things that you need," said the Professor, shaking Travis' hand and turning back to his trolley. He sped out of the little village across the rolling fields to the north, his mind puzzling over securing the grid with the strange machines and instruments in his workshop beneath the observatory.

He drove into the yard and noticed that the front door was standing open. Nobody on the island ever locked their doors but Ester always insisted that the door remain closed. "It's only proper," she would say. "Can't have folk wandering in unannounced, even though they do it all the time anyway."

He jumped out of the red trolley and hurried inside. The parlor was a shambles, the cages knocked over and the hawks were squawking loudly. The furniture was upended and only the two snake cages remained untouched. "Ester!" he yelled…"ESTER!"

Tic meowed feebly…Ponte turned to find the source of the sound. "Meow," again. He lifted the sofa and found Tic trapped underneath. The Professor reached down and gently cradled the cat, his pupils growing from tiny slits to full black and back again and blood was gushing from a slash on his left flank.

"What's happened? Where's Ester?"

"The Others…eight guards in black uniforms burst through the door demanding Alius. Ester told them that she wasn't here. They searched the house and, when they didn't find anything, they decided to take Ester as a hostage. I tried to help her but one of them got me with his dagger. I'm so sorry Professor."

"Oh, don't blame yourself, there was nothing that you could have done. We need to find some help and get you to Dr. Stevens. Do you think you can handle the ride?"

"I'm weak, but let's go!"

The Professor walked over to the cages and opened the latches, freeing the birds and then the snakes. "All of you…follow them, find out where they've gone and send a message to the House of the Four Seasons as soon as you know something."

Each of the hawks picked up a snake and flew out the front door. Professor Ponte wrapped Tic in a throw-blanket and carried him to the trolley. He placed the old cat gently in the wingback chair, climbed in the other side, turned the vehicle south, and pushed the pedal to the floor.

Magnus flew south, over the forest. He could see the little houses scattered to the east and west but there were no people along the paths or working in the fields. Finally, he spied the wagon, parked on the east side of the forest and swooped down to see if anyone was near.

Adrian, Alius, Molly, and Megan huddled in their favorite place, basking on the rocks in the stream, sharing corn, nuts, and cookies with the animals. Beggar was making every effort to steal food from the other critters gathered along the banks of the stream. Daphne snuggled Alius, who smiled brightly. "This is so wonderful," she said quietly. "I never knew this was possible."

"It isn't possible in the real world. This is The Balance, the magic of this place. I knew you'd understand, once you had a chance to meet our friends and to see the way our relationship with the animals should be."

Alius looked around and noticed a carpet of tiny green flowers growing at the base of the rock, "Do you know what these little flowers are? I've seen them growing on the other side of the mountain and they really stink."

Megan slipped off the boulder and knelt down to pick one but, before her fingertips touched the petite petals, the green mass expelled a pungent green mist. She fell over backwards, "Agh! They smell horrible!"

"Then leave them alone," laughed Molly.

"Guess that answers that question," said Adrian. "We obviously don't know a thing about this plant."

Alius stroked Daphne behind the ear, with one hand, and fed her corn with the other. Molly and Megan dropped nuts on the tummies of two raccoons, sprawled on their backs in a warm pool of sunshine. A rush of wings and a flash of golden feathers above the stream broke the serenity as Magnus landed on a large boulder, panting for breath, "They've taken Ester!"

Adrian turned and limped over to the rock beneath the giant bird, "Who did what?"

"The Others. I saw eight figures dressed in black cloaks enter the Professor's house and they came out with Ester. They headed north, back to the mountain," said Magnus, his golden eyes blazing and wings flapping frantically.

The children's eyes turned to Adrian, no one knowing quite what to say or do. He yelled, "We have to go now!" They abandoned the basket and clambered up the trail towards the wagon. Adrian turned back to the group of animals following after the children in confusion, "Meet us at the House of the Four Seasons. I hate to ask for your help again but we have to rescue Ester."

Alius stumbled after Molly and Megan up the path, wheezing, "This is all my fault...they wanted me, not Ester. Oh, not Ester!"

Adrian grabbed Alius, "This is not your fault but there will be something you can do to help get her back. Are you with us?"

Alius looked into his eyes. She was crying. "Yes, I'll do anything. Whatever needs to be done to get her back."

"Fine, then. Let's go."

They dashed up the trail, out of the forest, and jumped into the wagon. Megan took the wheel, peeled around, and raced along the path up the coast to the north.

The two vehicles almost collided as they swerved into the gate at the House of the Four Seasons...the Professor heading south, the children speeding north. The trolleys screeched to a stop at the steps to the kitchen door and the Professor hurried around to the other side of the red trolley and gently gathered Tic in his arms. The children ran over to him. "They've taken Ester!" said the Professor, "and Tic's been injured, he needs to see Dr. Stevens as soon as possible. Would one of you run him down to the doctor's house?"

"We will," said Molly as she took Tic from the Professor's arms and ran back to the wagon. Megan took the wheel and sped through the gate.

"We know what's happened. Magnus found us in the forest. He saw the whole thing. I'm sure he'll be along shortly," said Adrian. "The animals are gathering and they'll meet us here."

"Good, good," stammered the Professor. "We must find a way to get her back. Come along, we'll see what George and Elsie think."

They burst through the kitchen door to find Elsie canning vegetables. "Where's George?" demanded Ponte, flushed and panting.

"He's out in the autumn fields. Why? What's happened?"

"The Others have taken Ester. They were hoping to retrieve Alius but she wasn't there, so they took Ester as a hostage."

"Oh, my!" whispered Elsie, wiping her hands on a towel. "Here, sit. I'll run and get George. I'll be right back."

Adrian, Alius, and Ponte took chairs at the kitchen table, stunned to silence by an inconceivable violence long alien to the island. Alius sobbing quietly, tears dripping between fingers covering her eyes.

The Professor patted her on the shoulder and said, "My dear, this is not your fault. I should have set up some proper security, although it never dawned on me that anything like this could happen. We'll find a way to get her back but, in the meantime, I'll need you to focus. We'll need your considerable talents."

Adrian found a tissue and handed it to Alius. She blew her nose and dried her tears. "They want me. I'll just go home and they'll set her free."

"We don't have any reason to believe that to be true. Yes, they want you. That is to our advantage, but we'll not trade you for Ester. That's not the best solution. If you decide to return to your people, it will be because that is your choice not because you are forced into that decision."

"I can make them understand, I know I can."

"We'll see…but, for the moment, we'll need to learn what you know about where they might have taken her and what kind of guard they will post. It was only a few days ago that your leader's objective was control of the entire island and we have no reason to believe that those goals have changed. For all we know, your unique station has made you into more than an incidental pawn in this game that they're playing."

Alius buried her face in her hands again and wept. Adrian put his arm around her shoulders and pulled her to him, "The Professor's right and you know that in your heart. You're a *seer* and we need your brain, your talents."

George and Elsie hurried through the west door into the kitchen. Elsie looked frantic and walked behind Alius and enveloped her in a gentle hug, "This is not your fault."

"Elsie gave me an overview, now someone tell me what actually happened," demanded George, with a concerned but controlled glare in his eye.

Everyone spoke at once until Ponte raised one finger, "A squad of others broke into the observatory, hoping to retrieve Alius. When they didn't find her, they took Ester. Tic was injured and Molly and Megan have taken him to Dr. Stevens. I sent the two hawks, Harry and Harriet, with the snakes to follow them and scout their movements."

George was silent for a moment before he spoke, "My first instinct is to make sure that they don't have an opportunity to take her off the island. My second is that they'll want to trade for Alius. I also think they'll want more than just getting Alius back to end this conflict. What, I'm not sure."

Alius looked up at George, tears streaming down her cheeks, "Trade me! I'll go willingly."

Ponte reached over and patted her slender hand, "We'll get to that. In the meantime, I'd like to know everything you can tell us about where they might take her…the layout of the interior of the mountain, the most secure zones, their strengths and weaknesses, their weaponry and defenses…anything that you might know will help us."

Alius sat up in her chair. She seemed even more petite but her eyes focused. She blew her nose in a tissue, offered by Elsie, and when she glanced up, everyone in the room was staring at her. The words rolled slowly, carefully like the steps of a deer walking silently through snow in the forest.

"The only outlet to this side of the island is a tunnel they carved through the rock and undeveloped paths to the east and the west and

I'm sure they'll have guards posted. Our world is built as a maze of catacombs, with tunnels channeled throughout the mountain. There are many different and separated levels and areas, like the school, the kitchens, storage rooms, mechanical rooms, a production wing, residential and recreational areas, but I would guess that they'll keep her in the Master's chambers, which are sealed off from the rest of the population. That's where they took me to study the Book of Knowledge. When I got bored with the book, I'd sneak out and explore the halls around my room. There are many chambers hidden behind a series of locked doors at the deepest point in the mountain.

Your comment, George, about them taking her someplace off the island strikes me as a real possibility. They didn't intend to take Ester. They wanted me. It will take them a little while to create an alternative plan. Surely, they'll know you're coming for her and they'll mount a sturdy defense. Knowing our leader, he may decide to use any attack as an excuse to invade the rest of the island. He has a small army ready to move on command. They've been training for months."

George was quiet for a moment, as he took a chair at the table and folded his arms across his chest, "I think the first thing we ought to do is to make sure they can't take Ester off the island."

Molly and Megan burst into the kitchen. Everyone stopped talking and turned to the commotion. Molly stammered, "Dr. Stevens says that Tic will recover. He's stitching him up and they'll be here as soon as he's finished."

"Girls, do you think that you could find Spot and Dusty? They always seem to show up at the beach when you two are there."

"Sure, why?" asked Megan.

"I have a preliminary plan and I'll need their help. Go find them and ask them to meet me in the harbor as soon as possible," said George. "Elsie, get on the *messenger* and ring up Travis. Tell him what's happened and that I'm on my way."

Elsie hurried out of the room to George's study. The twins ran back through the kitchen door, jumped into the wagon, and headed south to bluff above the crescent beach.

"Professor, I want you to take our young *seers* to the observatory. First, we'll need an accurate map of the north side of the island. Second, I want you to explore the possibility of undoing Adrian's success of the other night. Is there any chance that changing the third crystal might disrupt their power supply?"

The Professor rose up in his chair, his mind focusing on the technical problems of manipulating the flow of The Powers, "You might be on to something. Although, as we've seen, there are dangers associated with disrupting the flow of energies from the Crystals. I'm confident that we'll find a solution to the problem with a bit of research."

"Good, just make it fast. I'll meet you there. In the meantime, I'll get Spot and Dusty to cripple their trawlers, so they can't take Ester off the island," said George.

"I think you'll have as much help as you need," said Dr. Stevens, as he stepped through the kitchen door with Tic in his arms. "I tried to convince Tic to stay at my place but he wouldn't have any part of it…and there's something that you should see outside."

The group rose from the kitchen table to follow him through the south door and each gasped in astonishment. The whole yard was filled with animals…Brandy and every dog that he could find, cats of every color, Daphne and her mate, Dante…raccoons…Beggar the bear and his family…Magnus sat on a branch in the tree beside the barn with his mate, more hawks, doves, hummingbirds, owls, cardinals, blue jays, seagulls, cranes, and every imaginable variety of bird…goats, cows, chickens, geese, ducks, turtles, horses, ponies, hedgehogs, rabbits, squirrels, fox, skunk, porcupines, possum, chipmunks, mountain lions, snakes, mice, frogs, gophers, with bees, wasps, mosquitoes, and flies hovering in giant swarms. Beyond the menagerie, the paths leading away from the House of the Four Seasons were jammed with more animals, all of them staring up at the small group of humans who had just emerged from the kitchen.

Tic purred in Dr. Steven's arms and said, "I think that we have an army, now we need a plan!"

Adrian stared at the swarms of insects buzzing around the porch for a long moment, turned to his Uncle George, "I think I know how to get Ester back without hurting anyone!"

Chapter Fourteen

The legion agreed to meet at the observatory after dark and the animals dispersed. George jumped into the trolley and tore down to the harbor to meet Travis and Spot and Dusty, who were playing around the pilings beneath the docks. The dock-master looked concerned, "What can I do to help?"

"I think we're on to a plan that might just work. Our first concern is that they don't have an opportunity to take Ester off the island and I think our friends here might be able to help."

"I'm at your service."

"Spot. Dusty, come here!" George yelled to the two dolphins, who swam over and sat up in the water like happy children awaiting a treat. "Ester's been kidnapped by the Others. Would you help us rescue her?"

"Of course," chirped Dusty.

"Here's the plan. We have lots of cables that were knocked down during the storm. I want you to follow Travis out to the waters just outside the cove on the north side of the island. Travis will give you pieces of cable and I want you to wrap them around the propellers on their trawlers, so that the boats can't be moved."

"We can do that!" smiled Spot.

"If you find any of their trawlers out of the harbor, I want you to locate and follow them. If they're all at their docks, then we know that Ester is still on the island."

The dolphins splashed and swam in circles, clicking madly.

"Travis, let's gather some of the cables that are lying about and load them on to the good trawler. Take her out to the north and find a blind spot where you know they can't detect you. Give the cables to our friends here, I think they know what to do."

"Right you are. Let's get moving," said Travis with a mischievous gleam in his eye.

Molly and Megan returned to the House of the Four Seasons with Joshua, Morgan, Ian, and Kelly. "We've found some volunteers!" cried Molly, as the group bounded through the back door.

Morgan hugged Adrian, "How are you two healing?"

"We'll be fine. We have more pressing matters to deal with and we sure can use your help," said the young *seer*, greeting his friends with hugs and handshakes. "We haven't quite got this all worked out but we will as soon as we can get to the Professor's house. In the meantime, would all of you help Elsie and Dr. Stevens and then meet us at the observatory after dusk?"

"Can I help too?" asked little Kelly, clutching to Adrian's good leg.

"Of course, I have a very special job for you."

Elsie and Dr. Stevens were busy packing food into baskets. It was going to be a long night and Elsie wanted to be sure that no one went into battle hungry.

Adrian and Alius followed the Professor out to his crazy red trolley but the boy stopped and looked at his companions, "I've just had two thoughts. First, Professor, if adults go in to find Ester, it's going to turn into a battle and I haven't seen a single weapon since I've been on the island, so I kind of doubt that anyone has any real military experience to mount a rescue, but...if children go in dressed as the children of the others, perhaps no one will notice. Second, Alius, if you go in with us and you're caught, the game's up."

Alius made no attempt to mask her disappointment, "I'll do whatever you ask but I'm the only one who knows how to get to where you want to go."

"I understand but I think I've got a way to get around it...do you agree?"

"We'll need dark clothing!" she said, running back into the house to tell the other children what to bring.

Harriet the hawk landed on the Professor's trolley, fluttering her wings and panting for air, "They took her into the tunnel. The snakes tried to follow but the guards chased them back out into the rocks with hissing seeker sticks. They've posted several sentries at the entrance of the tunnel and they're watching the south side of the island with a scope."

"Thank you, Harriet. Where's Harry?"

"He's flying reconnaissance above the entrance," she replied, fluttering. "I should relieve him."

"We'll be meeting at the observatory at dark," said Adrian as he stroked her feathers and felt her heaving to fill her lungs. "Why don't you rest for a moment before you return?" The hawk brushed up against his chest and looked up into his eyes, the warmth and determination of The Balance in her caress.

The afternoon was waning by the time the red trolley arrived at the observatory. The Professor parked the strange vehicle at an odd angle to the front door, blocking the view from the north. Adrian enveloped Alius in an old coat and ran into the house. They stumbled through the shambles in the parlor and took their places at the dining room table, where the Professor laid out the Book of Wisdoms.

He brought out pens and paper and placed them before Alius, "First, we need an accurate map of the north side of the island. Second, an estimate of their strengths and, if you think of any weaknesses or accesses or blind spots, those too."

"I can do this!" said Alius brightly, reaching for a pen to begin a sketch.

"Adrian, you understand how this book works. Let us begin with a question about their power grid."

The Professor opened the book and Adrian stared at the figures moving in random patterns across the glass pages.

Alius stopped drawing and looked up at Adrian and the Professor, "That's exactly like the Book of Knowledge. The figures are the same but it doesn't feel cold."

Ponte smiled, "The Texts hold all of the knowledge and the history of the Powers, both positive or negative. I have to believe that they are inherently neither good nor evil but each draws on a different energy and thus serves the interests of those of the dark and the light. They simply offer information that is dependent on the questions being asked. I wonder whether we might someday have both Books to work with, each drawing on the powers that run through those different vectors? That would be interesting, especially with two *seers*!"

Adrian turned back to the Book and asked, "Is there a way to disrupt the power grid on the north side of the island?"

The figures hesitated for a moment and then moved rapidly to form the word "Yes."

"Does it involve replacing the third crystal?"

"Yes."

"What do we replace the third crystal with?"

The figures moved and stopped, moved and stopped. Finally, they formed a golden crystal.

Adrian looked up at the Professor and Alius, who stopped drawing with a curious glance at Adrian and the Book. His face paled, for he knew what was being asked and he had not relished the sheer terror of his last visit to the Golden Crystal, which, he believed, almost killed him.

The Professor put his chubby hand on Adrian's shoulder and looked down at him, "Are you sure that you have the energy for this?"

"Once again, Professor, there is no other choice."

"Come along, children," sighed the Professor as he toddled to the elevator.

They descended to the cavern beneath the observatory. The doors parted into the white room bathed in the blinding glow of the giant spinning Crystal. The stone was moving very smoothly and Adrian felt that it was not quite as intimidating as the last time he had been in this room. Alius looked up at The Golden Crystal and her eyes opened very wide, "They never let me see The Black Crystal."

"We hope that you never have a reason to do what I'm about to do!" whispered Adrian with more than a little anguish.

He handed his crutches to Alius and crawled beneath The Crystal, brushed away the gold dust to reveal the slot, and inserted his key. A voice asked, "Who seeks entry?"

"I am Adrian, I am a *seer*."

"Back so soon?"

"I have several questions. May I enter The Crystal?"

"Yes, you may…if you are strong enough!"

The dark spot slowly spread up the spinning shards of crystal, a dark cloud surrounded by a blazing halo. The jewel gained speed and the air swirled around the room chasing the movements of the golden gem. Adrian's blond hair blew about his face as he turned to look back at the Professor and Alius, who held her hands over her ears and her mouth open, as if she was about to say something, but Adrian could not hear anything above the din of rushing air and energies. He turned back to the hole growing before him and the voice said, "You will enter The Crystal now!" He took a deep breath and stepped inside.

Again, the young *seer* found himself standing on the very small slab with The Crystal whirling around him at an astonishing speed. In the moment that his eyes adjusted, the strange figures marched out of the glare, up and down, around in every direction in organized chaos. The globe appeared and the continents spread apart. "How may we help you?" asked the voice.

"Is there a way to disrupt the power supplied by The Black Crystal?"

"There is."

"How would I accomplish this task?"

"First, you must understand that if you disrupt the power of The Black Crystal, you also interrupt the power of The Golden Crystal. They are perpetually tied together."

"I understand."

"Second, the system has not recovered from the recent turmoil, so, if the grid is not returned to normal within the hour, both Crystals will fail."

"I understand."

"Do you realize that any mistake will result in an end to The Balance?"

"Yes," said Adrian.

"Then let us proceed. Only a *seer* can accomplish this task. You will need an exact duplicate of the rainbow crystal that you installed recently. It must not be of crystalline form, although it would be preferable if the substance was derived from living matter."

"Are metals crystalline?"

"Yes, they are. Next, remove the rainbow crystal, in the same way that you removed the black crystal, and replace it with the substitute. From that moment, you will have exactly one hour, during which no power will be produced on the island. With each passing moment, The Black Crystal and The Golden Crystal will loose momentum. You must remove the substitute and insert the rainbow crystal before the hour is finished or any hope of restoring the grid will be lost and The Black and Golden Crystals will disintegrate. The Balance on this island will be lost forever."

Adrian was silent for a long moment, while he thought about the process just been described to him. "I believe that I understand the progression. Is there anything else that I should know?"

"Yes. This is a very dangerous procedure and, if you fail, there will be one less oasis on earth where The Balance can exist. There are too few of these sanctuaries left and when they are gone, life as you know it will perish."

"I would do nothing to endanger The Balance but there is one more thing that I need to ask about this procedure. Can another *seer* accomplish this task?"

"There is only one *seer* on this side of the island."

Adrian hesitated for a moment. "No. There are two. The *seer* from the north side of the island has joined with me."

"Is this not the one who tried to disrupt The Powers so recently?"

"Yes, she is. I believe now she understands The Balance and that she will work with us, rather than against us."

"This is most unusual. If she fails or turns back to her dark allegiances, all will be lost."

"I have no other choice than placing my faith in her."

"We believe that you are sincere. If there was any other way to accomplish your goals, you would not be asking these questions."

"A very special life depends on the outcome of this process."

"Very well. Is there anything else that we might help you with?"

"Yes. May I see the globe that you showed me the last time? I'm most interested in the area the north of the equator in the eastern Pacific Ocean."

Slowly, the figures marching in strange formations moved away and a globe began to spin very slowly. Again, a giant continent appeared and the pieces floated apart. Tiny red lights glowed, here and there, across the surface and, one by one, disappeared, leaving fewer glowing dots. The globe stopped spinning as the western Pacific came into view. There, just off the coast of Mexico, a single red dot glowed brightly next to a black point. Adrian could feel the energy draining from his body but he smiled to himself, "I know where they are!"

"Thank you for your instruction. I will be very careful to accomplish the task that we discussed, as you've instructed."

The globe disappeared and the figures returned to their marching.

"The Balance is in your hands. Do not fail. You may leave now," said the voice. The dark spot appeared to Adrian's right and he stepped through it to find Alius and the Professor standing exactly where they were when he entered. Alius' mouth was still open.

Adrian smiled at the Professor, fell to his knees and slowly leaned forward until his forehead thumped the floor. Alius and Ponte rushed forward to catch him.

"I don't believe what I just saw you do. Are you alright?" asked the little *seer*.

"It takes an incredible amount of energy. I feel weak but I'll be better in a little while. In the meantime, I know how to do this. Professor, The Crystal told me to replace the rainbow Crystal with a substitute. It must not be of crystalline form and it would be better if it were made of living matter."

"Ah, I have just the thing. I use a wooden duplicate to size the receptacles in my machines. It's a bit worn but it should do nicely. Sit down for a moment and rest. I'll just go to my tool room to fetch it."

Alius sat down next to Adrian and pulled the bandage off her head. She had a huge bruise on her temple. Adrian reached up and touched it gently. "I'm sorry."

She brushed the gold dust off his face, "What happened in there?"

"I asked some questions and the voice answered me. I know how to turn off all the power on the island but you and I are the only ones who can remove the rainbow Crystal. I can't climb that mountain. You can. There is one stipulation, once the rainbow Crystal is removed, it must be replaced within one hour. If we don't get it reconnected within that time, The Balance and the Powers will be lost forever."

Alius looked deeply into his eyes and then up at the spinning Golden Crystal, "A week ago, I couldn't have understood or appreciated any of this. My mission was to disrupt The Balance, to take back all that had been stolen from my people. Now it has become something that I would give my life to protect, something our people should share together."

Chapter Fifteen

Alius finished the last details of the map, just as George, Elsie, Dr. Stevens, Tic and the other children arrived at the observatory. Adrian dragged himself off the couch and hobbled to the group gathered around the dining room table to inspect the diagram.

"There are only two ways to get into the tunnels, three large arches on the north side facing the harbor and the tunnel that leads in from the south side of the mountain. There are three primary sectors that need to be explored. I've marked those in red. The most obvious are the Master's Chambers. They're buried behind the mechanical rooms deep inside the mountain. They'll also be the hardest to reach because you'll have to follow the new tunnel from the south side of the mountain all the way to the harbor entrance and then turn back through the central wing. The passageways are sealed with locks that require special keys, like the one I carry," said Alius, pulling the triangular key from her pocket. "I know this key will open the doors leading out but I don't know if it will open the locks leading in. I was never allowed into those chambers without an escort…and the deeper you go, the more dangerous the energies of the Dark Crystal will be."

"I would suggest checking these other tunnels that lead from the harbor entrance to the southeast and the southwest. This one on the east leads to the kitchens, the school, and the residences, there are only a few secure areas but they're worth checking. The other one, to the west, leads to the workshops and the production zone." She looked up at the faces peering down at the drawing. They all smiled.

George asked, "What about air flow…how is air pumped in and out of the tunnels and the rooms around them?"

"There are large ducts running through all of the tunnels with intakes on either side of the main entrance on the north and, if I remember, there are also large grates on the east and the west."

"And their strengths and weaknesses?" inquired George quietly.

"At the moment, I would guess there are more than five hundred men, not quite as many women, and seventy-five or eighty children. Their strength lies in their training and their dedication to the Masters. Their weakness is the same thing. They've been trained to follow orders, not to think for themselves. I'd guess pandemonium would erupt in an unusual situation. They've never had to actually fight anyone. The primary mission of the guards is to keep the rest of us under control."

George looked concerned but remained silent.

Adrian leaned against the table, "I suggested to the Professor that if adults go into that complex, there will be a battle and many people on both sides will be hurt. We don't possess any real weapons and no one, on this side of the island, has been trained in any sort of combat. We have enough young people here to cover all these areas and I'm hoping that, if we can cause enough commotion, they might not notice that we don't belong."

George looked at each of the children in turn, "Are each of you sure that you want to do this?"

"Yes!" they cried in unison.

"Kelly, you'll be in charge of the stampede," said Adrian, "one of the most important jobs. Do you think you can handle it?"

"I can do it!" squealed Kelly.

"Alright. Molly, you go with Josh and cover the east tunnel. Megan, you and Ian scout the west. Morgan, you and I will try to get into the Master's Chambers. Alius, you're on the mountain. Take Brandy with you, he can show you the path I followed last week which should be a bit easier without the blizzard and some crazy girl with a knife. We'll need at least five watches."

Each of the adults took off their watches and handed them out. They were one short. The Professor hustled out of the room and returned with a watch that Ester kept beside her bed...she had not put it on this morning…and gave it to Alius. Dr. Stevens handed his pocket watch to little Kelly and hooked the chain around her neck, "Don't drop this, it is very old and very special to me. Do you know how to tell time?"

"Yes, and I won't drop it. I'll be very careful and return it to you when we get Ester back." Kelly held the watch with both hands and looked down at the ornate face, "It says it's nine o'clock!"

"Do all the watches agree?"

They all chimed in, "Yes."

"Then let's plan to move in at midnight. Alius, it will take at least an hour for you to get to the knot, so you can replace the crystal at exactly midnight. Kelly will send in the flies at about eleven-thirty, then the mosquitoes and bees at five minutes before the hour. We'll let the first wave of animals go at midnight and we'll go in with the second, a few minutes later," said Adrian. Everyone nodded in agreement.

George turned to the Professor, "Do you have anything we could use as a distraction?"

The Professor's face lit up with an impish grin, "Oh, I certainly do. It will give the adults something to contribute!" He rushed out of the room, into the elevator, and disappeared. After a few minutes, he reappeared dragging several large cartons out of the little cab.

Leaning into the largest crate to retrieve a sample, he giggled like a schoolboy, "First, I found these flash pans. They're so bright they'll blind anyone looking directly at them for a few minutes. Each group of children should take a few of these along, although I hope that you have no need to use them. They go off with a mighty flash ten seconds after you pull the string. Just be sure that you cover your eyes as you set them off or they'll blind you too."

He handed several to each of the young invaders. They were about the size of an apple and covered in silver foil, with a string hanging out where a stem might reside. "I also have some high intensity *orbs* that will light your way," Ponte lit up a broad grin, "and…I've been making fireworks for the next festival. I suppose they'll be just as much fun tonight and our belligerent neighbors will certainly be entertained!"

George took charge, "Right then. Doc, you and Kelly will be in charge of the animals. Professor, you take a box of fireworks to the west and I'll take a box to the east. Elsie, would you run a box down to Travis and have him cruise around to the harbor entrance. He should be back at the village by now. At midnight, everyone start setting them off. Aim them above the entrances! That should provide a beautiful diversion."

"Children, go change into your dark clothes, they'll allow you to blend in a little. I'm sorry we didn't have any black leather uniforms but...?" said Elsie. "I have food for everyone in the kitchen!"

The children filed into the next room and returned moments later. There was nothing they could do about the color of their hair but hope that, in the chaos about to unfold, it would not matter.

They emerged from the observatory to find hundreds of animals waiting silently in the meadow to the south. The Doctor held Tic in his arms.

The old cat scanned his comrades, "My friends, we are on a mission to retrieve Ester and we have a plan. First, flies...enter every entrance to the tunnels and the air ducts on the north side of the island, explore every room, every nook where they might be keeping Ester. Report back to the children, who will follow you in the third wave into the tunnel bored in the south side of the mountain."

"Next, mosquitoes, bees and wasps...at five minutes before midnight, Kelly and Dr. Stevens will give you the signal to enter the tunnels and push the guards back. You'll be followed by all of the small animals...the mice, rats, skunks, raccoons, possum, rabbits, squirrels, and porcupines will lead the way. Third, the larger animals will then escort the children to their destinations. When Ester has been found, all of you will surround Ester and our children and lead them back out through the south tunnel. We would prefer that no one, on either side, gets hurt in this expedition. Are there any questions?"

There were murmurs, grunts, whinnies, moos, and every sort of animal sound, but they were all in agreement.

Bessie, the mule, moved to the front of the group and said, "Adrian is still on crutches and he's limping. I can carry two of you and I think the horses could each carry two of the other children, you're all fairly small, if that would help? We're sure-footed and we'll help you move faster than you might on your own."

"That's a great idea," said Adrian. "It would help if one of you could take Alius to the base of the mountain. She has a special job to do. Brandy, are your paws healed enough to lead her to the knot?"

"Certainly," said Brandy, who was sitting to one side. "I would be honored!"

Alius walked over to Brandy and knelt down beside him. "Friends?" she asked.

"If you're with us, then you're a friend."

Adrian walked over as she hugged the red dog, "We should exchange keys."

Alius pulled the triangular key from her pocket and accepted his.

"Oh, one more thing. The Professor gave us some flashpans that make a blinding flash, so when I yell 'eyes', everyone close your eyes.

"Right then, places everyone. This is going to be a long night!" said George.

Ester shivered, sitting alone in the cold dark room, under the deep purple glow of a single *orb* suspended in the ceiling. She decided the light made her skin look frightfully pallid and she would be spending more time in the sunlight when she escaped this horrid dungeon.

The group of large men, in black leather uniforms, broke into the house, looking for Alius. Not finding her, they hauled Ester up the side of the mountain, through dark tunnels, and deposited her in this room. She assumed that it might be used as a very small study or classroom, as there were several desks and chairs, and a blackboard attached to one wall.

The mechanical hum of the air-conditioning whistled through two vents in the room, one in the ceiling and the other high up on the wall near the door, a white noise blocking any sound from outside. She pushed one of the desks beneath the vent, climbed on top, and stood on her tiptoes but the outlet was sealed from behind the wall and she doubted that she could have pulled herself through the small shaft, even if she found some way to pry it open.

No one had been back to check on her since the door slammed and the lock clicked into place. She needed to use a bathroom and she was hungry and thirsty but she was not about to show any weakness to these...heathens.

The hypnotic rush of air was disrupted by the faint buzzing of two flies whizzing around her head. She waved her hand to brush them away but they persisted in flying near her face. One of the flies landed on her hair near her left ear and she thought she heard it buzz, "They're coming for you."

"Oh, it's just my imagination," she thought, waving her hand again, but the two flies landed on the desk in front of her. They stood on their hind legs and waved their wings in unison, buzzing frantically. She watched, mesmerized, as one of the flies flew out through the larger vent in the ceiling and the other darted under the crack at the bottom of the door and it was quiet again. "Not only am I hungry, thirsty, in need of a bathroom...and I'm losing my mind!"

The two guards at the entrance to the tunnel in the south side of the mountain were bored and tired. It was dark and, other than the

Professor's red trolley, which arrived at the observatory hours ago, nothing seemed to be moving in the darkness on the south side of the island.

"Are they ever going to relieve us? I'm hungry," grumbled one of the guards to the other.

"I'll go find you something to eat, if you like," said the second guard.

"You're not leaving me alone out here!"

"Well then, we're stuck until we're relieved," said the second sentry, swatting at a mosquito flying around his face. Suddenly both men were swinging their arms wildly, as bees, wasps, and mosquitoes buzzed around their heads and burrowed beneath their clothing. They stumbled into the tunnel to escape the swarm but the cloud of insects persisted.

Hundreds of mice and rats scurried through the tunnel in a furry stampede. Groups of rodents split off to check every nook and cranny they encountered, followed by a wave of raccoons, possum, rabbits, skunks, squirrels, chipmunks, and porcupines.

At the north entrance, the guards began swatting at swarms of mosquitoes, bees, and wasps that clouded the light from the massive *orbs* over the triple arches. They jumped up and down as mice and rats scampered around their feet. Over their heads, the sky lit up with brilliant explosions. Citizens streamed through the tunnel entrances screaming about skunks spraying everyone they encountered and porcupines firing quills at anything that moved. Two eagles, several hawks, and hundreds of other birds swooped down on the population exiting the tunnels, driving them away to either side of the quay.

At that moment, all the lights dimmed and the faint purple glow of emergency lights provided only dim illumination. The tunnels suddenly overflowed with animals charging in all directions, chasing every human to the north entrances. Dogs, cats, fox, geese, ducks, birds, and their comrades joined the rodents. Goats, sheep, two large deer, bears, four or five mountain lions, a few ponies, two horses, and a mule followed the smaller animals. In their panic, no one noticed the children clinging to the backs of these foreign and frightening creatures.

The Masters stormed out of chambers, screaming for the guards to regain control, but insects and animals scampering through every open space overwhelmed them. The animals drove deeper and deeper into the maze of tunnels and chambers inside the mountain. Within minutes, the entire community within the mountain was herded through the north entrance and pinned under a barrage of fireworks that George, the Professor, and Travis were gleefully firing over their heads. The skies blazed with explosions of every imaginable color and showers of sparks cascaded down the rocks above shrieking darts skittered along the wharf.

Molly and Josh were riding on the back of Sanchez, a large chestnut stallion, and turned east at the base of the south tunnel to explore the residences, the kitchen, and the classrooms. Megan and Ian veered into the west tunnel, where they found workshops and the production facilities. Morgan slid from Bessie's back and led the mule and Adrian around to the south into the mechanical wing. A fly landed on Adrian's nose and buzzed loudly, "This way, this way!"

They passed along a broad concourse through the cavernous mechanical heart of the complex, giant machines, now silent, burrowed into alcoves bored into dark stone. The cavern narrowed through a series of gleaming metal locks and, finally, two heavy metallic doors, engraved with a giant dragon stood ajar. A violent chill raced up his spine and crashed into the base of his skull, as he dismounted and left Bessie at the entrance. The Professor's *orbs* cut through the darkness at the center of the room where they found a large round table with five chairs facing the entrance in disarray. They passed around the table into a long hallway and a series of doors that were closed and locked.

Morgan's teeth were chattering as she knocked on the first door to the left. There was no response. They hammered on the second door with the same result but when they pounded on the third door, someone banged back from the other side. Adrian glanced at Morgan, whose lips were blue, "Ester! Ester! Are you there?"

A muffled voice carried through the steel, "Help."

Adrian withdrew Alius' triangular key and inserted it in the slot. The door opened and their *orbs* licked through the crack, illuminating Ester, shielding her eyes and looking slightly bewildered. Her blue dress was tattered and her hair was a mess.

They pushed into the room and wrapped their arms around her. "Let's go, we don't have much time!" urged Morgan.

The children escorted her out through the Masters' chamber, then the double doors, and lifted her onto Bessie's back. Morgan grabbed the reins and led the mule out through the mechanical wing until they reached the tunnel to the south. "You take her out of here and I'll go find the Molly and Megan," shouted Adrian, limping past the central arch framing a barrage of colored explosions.

"Are you sure you're alright?" asked Morgan.

"Just get her out of here, we'll be along in a minute."

Adrian hobbled to the tunnel leading off to the west and whistled. He could see *orbs* flashing as Megan and Ian appeared out of the darkness, "We found her, get out of here!"

"No, you get out of here, we'll find Josh and Molly."

"Then we'll all go together!"

Josh and Molly rode into the east tunnel, only to turn around as Megan and Ian cantered out shouting, "A dove said you found her, is she okay?"

Adrian put his fingers in his mouth and whistled again. All of the animals, still bounding in all directions, suddenly turned back into the south tunnel and surrounded the children. Adrian yelled, "Everyone close your eyes for a moment!" as Josh, Molly, Megan, and Ian pulled flash pans from their pockets and tossed them through the arches producing a series of intense bursts, followed by panicked screams.

Dante pushed his way into the throng and brushed up against Adrian, "You'll slow us down, climb on my back and hold on tight!"

Adrian jumped and swung his injured leg over Dante's back,

"Am I too heavy?"

"You're fine, just hold on and I'll get you out of here."

Alius pulled Brandy closer in the darkness. Stars twinkled over the island and a chilling wind blew in from the east. All the lights on the south end of the island were extinguished when she replaced the rainbow crystal with the wooden spacer. She kept checking her watch and knew that she had to replace the crystal within the next few minutes, "I sure hope you guys found Ester because time is running out."

Out of the darkness, she heard a swish in the air, a rustle of wings above her head. Magnus landed on the rock just above the crystals, "They've got Ester. Adrian said go ahead!"

The eagle squawked and flew up in the air, swooping down to Alius' right with his talons extended to attack. Brandy raised his nose to sniff a new scent in the night air, crouched, and growled a warning. Alius spun to her right to find Jofre standing over her. Brandy barked and she grabbed him just as he reared back to leap, "Brandy, No!"

Magnus made another pass at the huge man, who ducked at the last moment, reached for his dagger, and swiped at the eagle.

"So it is you!" shouted Jofre, venom raging in his voice. His white eyes blazed in the darkness, "Somehow, I knew you were the only one who could shut down the power. You're our *seer*. How could you join with the enemy against us?"

Alius held Brandy with both hands but the dog was dragging her across the slick rocks, trying to attack, "Brandy! Stop it! Magnus, come here!"

Brandy turned to Alius, hackles up and teeth bared. Magnus returned to his perch above the crystals but kept his wings away from his body, ready to fly to the attack.

Alius looked down at her watch. The hour had almost passed,

"I'll explain it to you and I'll restore the power to the island…but you'll have to wait for a few minutes, while I do this."

Jofre reached down, seething with anger, and grabbed her arm. Brandy growled and snapped at him. The huge man let go of the girl and swiped his blade at Brandy, who ducked, snarling, ready to spring.

Alius jumped to her feet and moved between the giant man and the growling red dog. "No!" she shouted. "This is the moment when our lives can change…the moment when our brothers and sisters can come out of the shadows but all will be lost for everyone on this island, unless you give me a few minutes to accomplish this task. Now back off! Brandy, sit and be quiet. You too, Magnus."

Brandy sat down between Alius and the Master with the white eyes, intent on Jofre's every move. He raised his ears and pulled his lips back in a threatening grimace. Magnus leaned forward, eager to fly.

Jofre could not fathom the transformation in the girl, she had been an obedient child, a talented and vigilant young *seer*, and she had never spoken to him in this tone. He was The Master of his people. He leaned forward again.

Brandy snarled, "I suggest that you give her a few minutes to do what she needs to do."

Jofre stared at the Irish setter and his jaw dropped open in astonishment. Accustomed to having his every decree followed precisely, he relied on discipline and duty. He expected those beneath him to view him with fear and respect and now he was expected to take orders from a talking dog?

He took a step back and Alius spun around and knelt before the wooden replica impaled in the slot between the four barely glowing crystals. She pressed the red gems in order…north, south, east, and west. The wooden spike rose out of the notch and she grabbed it, inserting the rainbow crystal that she took from a piece of cloth.

The little *seer* pressed each crystal in reverse order…west, east, south, north, and the rainbow crystal began to descend into the crevice and then stopped. She turned to Brandy in a panic then pressed the four red crystals again. Nothing happened. Time was running out.

She sat back on her haunches and stared at the half-submerged crystal. She tried to pull up on the gemstone but it would not budge. She pressed down and still, it did not move. Her hands were shaking, her promise to Adrian ringing through her mind.

"I need your help."

Jofre moved closer. Brandy leaned forward in a threatening crouch and watched Jofre's white eyes.

"Brandy, we have no choice. I need another hand to help me with the crystal and you don't have hands, you have paws. Let him approach."

Brandy sat down, as Jofre knelt beside her.

"The crystal is stuck. If I can't move it into place, all the power on the island will be lost forever. That will be the end for our people and for those who live on the south side of the island. Will you help me?"

"Yes," said Jofre. He had never allowed anyone to direct his actions. This was the first moment in his life when he had not been in complete control and he suddenly realized that everything he tried to accomplish for his people could disintegrate if he did not assist his young *seer* with this task in the next few moments.

Alius pressed the crystals in the first order - north, south, east, west…the crystal emerged. She removed it from its mount and used the cloth to clean it very carefully. She lit her *orb* and stared down into the mount, spying a splinter sticking up from the bottom of the crevice. She turned to Jofre and handed him the crystal, "Hold this and don't drop it. It's the crystal that will balance the power between the Golden Crystal and the Black Crystal and I don't have another."

He reached out to take the crystal and held it carefully. It was the first time that she had ever seen him use such a gentle touch.

She reached her fingers down into the clasp but could not quite reach the splinter, fuming, "I need a pair of tweezers!"

Jofre held the crystal in one hand and withdrew a huge dagger from a scabbard on his leg. Brandy's ears perked up. "Here, hold the crystal for a moment," he said, handing the gem back to Alius.

He unscrewed the handle of the knife and withdrew a long slender blade, "It's not tweezers but perhaps it might help." He handed the thin stiletto to the girl and Brandy relaxed.

Alius returned the rainbow crystal and inserted the blade into the slot, wiggling it around several times. "Almost," she said very quietly, her electric blue eyes focused in total concentration. After several tries, she pulled the blade from the opening very slowly, balancing the small piece of wood on the tip, "Give me the crystal!"

He handed the shimmering stone to her, took the blade, and replaced it in the handle of his knife.

Alius inserted the crystal and pressed the four red gems in reverse order. The stone descended into the slot and began to glow dimly at first, then brighter and brighter. Alius smiled, withdrew Adrian's key, and sat back against the boulder. She hugged Brandy and turned to the giant man, "Thank you."

"You're welcome…but, in spite of dashing our plans, I think it is I who should be thanking you," he said, moving to sit beside her. He was an enormous man and Alius felt very small next to him. They looked out into the darkness over the south side of the island as, one by one, lights began to flicker on in farmhouses scattered here and there in a patchwork of fields.

Alius said, "Magnus, fly to Adrian. Tell him that the mission is accomplished. The rainbow crystal is balancing the other two!"

"If you're sure you'll be safe?" The eagle looked down into her smile, raised his wings and disappeared into the darkness.

Jofre watched the eagle fly off into the night and turned to the beautiful young *seer*, "I want to be angry with you but I'm afraid, I don't know what I feel at the moment." He reached out to pet Brandy and the red dog licked his hand, his first gentle encounter with an animal, let alone a dog that could speak.

"In the few days that I've spent with these people, I've learned many things and there's much more I want to understand. I've realized that, in many ways, they're like us but they're happy. They've harnessed the Powers that exist on this island and turned this small patch of land into a paradise because they work hard. The reason for their success is their belief in what they call The Balance.

Where we've been taught to extract every resource from the land for our own purposes, they believe they're sharing the land with all the other creatures who live on this island. There is no killing. Animals are not slaughtered for food for the humans. Rather, all of the animals are held in high esteem…they are partners in maintaining this very special place."

Jofre was silent for a few minutes, staring out into the night, then drew a deep breath, "We will see what comes of it…"

"How long have the two sides suffered this separation?" continued Alius. "How many generations have passed since our ancestors started boring tunnels into the north side of the island?"

"It's been hundreds of years."

"Does anyone on either side remember why the separation occurred in the first place? Does it matter any longer? Why must we continue to relive our ancestors' mistakes? This is the moment to renew our relationship with these people. We're all of the same families. All of us are descendants of those who accompanied Morgan in those first ships. Adrian, the boy who is the *seer* for the people of the south, has my eyes. We could be cousins."

They were quiet again, lost in their thoughts. Brandy raised his head, as Harry and Harriet landed on the rocks above them. A mountain lion emerged from the darkness and sat down beside Alius, followed by chipmunks, squirrels, fox, several goats, a family of rabbits, and two young deer. Jofre looked concerned at the small menagerie surrounding them. Alius smiled and hugged his arm, "This is The Balance."

Chapter Sixteen

Ester dismounted from Bessie and ran into Ponte's open arms. The children and a massive herd of animals marched down the trail from the mountain, spewing out across the barren field to surround them like water flooding into a barren lake from a rain sodden stream. George, Elsie, and Travis pulled up to the group in the trolley.

Little Kelly took the pocket watch hanging from her neck and held it up to Dr. Stevens. "How'd I do?"

The Doctor took the watch from Kelly and held the antique timepiece up to admire it, "You did a great job. Everyone moved right on schedule and no one got hurt. I'd say that qualifies as a complete success! I told you that this watch is very special to me. I want you to have it. You've earned it."

The Doctor looped the golden chain around her neck and gave her a gentle pat on the back. Holding the pocket watch with both hands, Kelly looked up beaming with pride. The Doctor leaned over and whispered, "When we have some time, I'll teach you about the special things this watch can do."

Adrian hugged Morgan and turned to the animals crowding the fields below the mountain. "Thank you all!" he shouted. The humans cheered and the animals made a deafening racket.

Magnus circled above the herd sweeping across the open fields to land on top of Ponte's red trolley, "Alius said to tell you that she has accomplished her mission. The crystal is back in place!"

Adrian walked over to the trolley and looked up at the beautiful eagle, "Where's Alius?"

"When I left, she was sitting with a huge man on the mountain." The eagle squinted into the darkness, "I think I'll let her explain it to you. Here she comes now!"

Alius strode out of the darkness leading Franklin, the beautiful stallion, followed by Brandy, and a very large man, dressed in a black leather uniform. The herd of animals parted as she walked to her new friends. Alius looked up at the huge man with the white eyes then turned to the crowd, "Everyone! I would like you to meet my father, Master of our Council, Jofre!"

The Characters

Adrian – son of John and Sara
John – Adrian's father
Sara – Adrian's mother
Stubby and Kick – friends from Heritage Academy

Morgan's Knot

George – Adrian's uncle
Elsie – George's wife, Sara's sister
Molly and Megan – twin daughters of Elsie and George
Morgan Keelty – Adrian's first new friend
Joshua Keelty – younger brother of Morgan
Ian Sheridan – Adrian's second cousin
Kelly Sheridan – Adrian's second cousin, younger sister of
        Ian
Spot and Dusty – dolphins
Professor Ponte – Keeper of the Powers, astronomer,
        teacher
Ester – Ponte's wife
Tic – Ponte and Ester's opinionated black and white tomcat
Brandy – Keelty's Irish setter
Travis – harbor-master
Dr. Stevens – physician
Patrick – friend of Molly & Megan
Daphne & Dante – deer
Damien – Daphne & Dante's foal
Beggar – small bear
Magnus – large male eagle
Harriet and Harry – hawks

The Others

Jofre – Master of the Council
Mandor – Head of production and security
Nanchez – Keeper of the Dark Powers
Alius – daughter of Jofre, dark *seer*
Sheridan – Alius' aunt

Atlantis

Jofre – powerful and wealthy merchant
Alius – glamorous single woman
Demetre – Alius' older brother, captain of the Jasmine
Simian – Alius' younger brother, scribe
Protus – Simian's friend, scribe
Modulus – Master Scribe
Nanu - Keeper of the Powers on Atlantis

Jamaica

Sammy – dockhand
Simian – Sammy's uncle, potential *seer*
Mona – Sammy's aunt

The Island of the Children

Morgan's Knot – A Serial Fantasy
Episode II

A blazing smudge of liquid orange splattered firelight across the indigo water as the sun melted into the Pacific. Roger Johnson sat on the aft deck of his new yacht, the Tigger Too, watching his children, Todd and Sandy, fishing off the stern. They were anchored in a small isolated cove near the Bahia de San Quintin for the night, on their first run down the Mexican coast. His latest screenplay earned him a small fortune and the new boat was a reward to himself. It was one of the fastest racers on the water and comfortably accommodated six in the luxurious cabin below decks.

His wife, Peggy, was cleaning up the dishes in the galley and popped out of the hatch, "Like a beer?"

"Sure," replied Roger with a broad smile. He felt like the Cheshire Cat, purring, *"Life is good."*

Peggy brought an icy bottle of Olympia to her husband, gave him a hug, and disappeared into the galley.

He called to his children, "Any bites?"

Todd turned and smiled, "Nothing yet, but I know they're down there!"

"You'll get one."

His daughter, Sandy, turned to her father, "Hey Dad, do you see that boat out there? It sure is coming fast!"

Roger gazed out through the mouth of the little cove. She was right, a boat was running wide open into the bay straight out of the last blazing wash of the sun. There were no running lights on the approaching craft and, as he watched, the hairs on the back of his neck began to prickle and a bead of cold sweat trickled down his cheek.

The boat turned hard at the last moment and settled next to the

Tigger2. The driver, wearing a brightly colored Hawaiian shirt and sunglasses over a three-day growth of stubble, called out in a heavy Spanish accent, "Hey, mind if we anchor on the other side of the cove?"

Roger stood up, waved at the man standing at the wheel of the mystery boat, and called, "No, we don't mind."

The pilot of the other boat gunned the engines and smiled, "Great! Hope we're not disturbing you."

"Not at all."

"Have you seen any other boats this evening?"

"No, we're here alone," yelled Roger.

The boat drifted closer to the Tigger2 and several other men appeared on the deck brandishing small machine guns.

The children dropped their fishing rods and ran to their father.

The pilot of the other boat called out, "We'll be boarding you. Do not resist or we'll shoot los ninos!"

Three men from the second boat jumped aboard and hustled Roger and his children below decks.

"We'll be taking your kids with us and you'll take my comrades where they ask to go or you'll never see them again!"

Roger had no weapons on board and knew that he was no match for these muscular young men. There was no defense. A voice called down through the hatch, "His tanks are full."

One of the men held a gun on Roger and Peggy, while the other two carried the screaming children up the ladder, tossed them on the other boat and down to the cabin below, where they were bound and gagged. The captain chuckled to one of the other men, "We can't harm the children. It's the pirate's code. We'll leave them on the island and meet you at the rendezvous."

One of the pirates returned to the Tigger2 and said, "Let's get moving."

The second boat headed west as the Tigger2 turned north.

The adventure continues in

The Island of the Children

Morgan's Knot - A Serial Fantasy
Episode II

Desperate to rescue his shipwrecked parents, Adrian and his friends embark on a journey to locate an uncharted island in the Pacific where they join a tribe of children and a troupe of circus animals to battle a brutal band of pirates.

Visit: www.morgansknot.com

Eric T. Stiller is the author of the Morgan's Knot Fantasy Serial as well as the adult novels in his Redemption Series. He is an award-winning commercial photographer, musician, and Master Gardener. Visit: www.rickstiller.com for more of his work.

If you enjoyed this story, please give it a five-star review on my Amazon sales page and like my 'Eric T Stiller – Author' page on Facebook.

Young Adult

Fiction

Visit: www.rickstiller.com for more of his books, photographs, and music and www.morgansknot.com for the latest on the Morgan's Knot series.

www.ingramcontent.com/pod-product-compliance
Lightning Source LLC
Chambersburg PA
CBHW050731250626
47155CB00005B/1754